Suicide Note
Of
The Father Of Punjab

Harsh K Arora

Ukiyoto Publishing

[Scan the QR Code to check for any special feature]

All global publishing rights are held by

Ukiyoto Publishing

Published in 2020

Content Copyright © **Harsh Kumar**

ISBN 9789364946636

All rights reserved.
No part of this publication may be reproduced, transmitted, or stored in a retrieval system, in any form by any means, electronic, mechanical, photocopying, recording or otherwise, without the prior permission of the publisher.

The moral right of the author has been asserted.

This is a work of fiction. Names, characters, businesses, places, events, locales, and incidents are either the products of the author's imagination or used in a fictitious manner. Any resemblance to actual persons, living or dead, or actual events is purely coincidental.

This book is sold subject to the condition that it shall not by way of trade or otherwise, be lent, resold, hired out or otherwise circulated, without the publisher's prior consent, in any form of binding or cover other than that in which it is published.

Dedicated To

Nature ji and Mummy ji

One for the readers' existence and the other for my existence

Acknowledgement

It all started with a belief that this world needs laughter more than logic. A belief ingrained in the DNA of a place which inarguably has the highest per capita fun in this world. Thank you, small towns of Punjab for sharing happy and carefree stories.

The art of storytelling is still alive, courtesy beer companies which make offline rendezvous of friends possible in today's digital world. Had it not been for the fun filled, nonstop nonsense evenings in Hyderabad, my stories would not have seen the light of the day. Long live Kingfisher beer and the Ling-Long gang!

This novel would have perpetually remained in the D: Drive of my laptop if not for the persistence and motivation of my wife, who to this day believes my fake stories to be true. Thank you, Megha.

The brain can think freely only if the ecosystem is supportive. Thank you Abohar family, especially dad and mom-in-law for not forcing me to be politically correct.

Lastly, Ukiyoto for endless threads of emails to make this a reality.

Disclaimer

The author has taken the liberty of using non-formal English at certain places to highlight the poor linguistic skills of the protagonist.

CONTENTS

To God Ji *1*

My Plan *14*

The Worst Mama Ji Of The World *45*

Abnormal School Life *70*

Sant Singh College, Abohar *106*

The Search Of Needs *134*

Canada - The Foundation Stone Of My Suicide *159*

Last Few Minutes Of My Life *206*

About the Author *211*

Cybercafé - Day I

To God Ji

19th November, 2010, 10:31:21 P.M.

Jagga's Cyber Café - Dangar Khera - Punjab - India - Earth - Milky Way - Something even bigger, maybe China

To
God Ji
Here/There/Everywhere/Nowhere

Subject: 'I am Fuck'

Sir/Madam,

    With due respect, I hereby state that I am a very handsome and smart young human being. Though I never worshipped you much in my life but I did not leave you alone in the times of my needs either, so that makes us good friends because I was taught in my English lessons in class 9th A that 'A friend in need is a friend indeed.'

Now that we are friends, I must admit that I am very much jealous of you because you are a 'real dude.' This does not mean that I am not a real dude but it's my honest obligation to flatter you a bit especially when I am a writer and you are a reader, otherwise why would you read the remaining of my letter? Now that you have been flattered, I will come to the real stuff. God ji, please don't think that my English is poor and I am using the same word 'real' again and again because normally my English is a real gem of a language. It's just that I am taking a little help from the green and red lines which appear under almost all the words while typing on this huge computer and sometimes I even refer to the English dictionary in this computer to find the real English words for their Punjabi counterparts.

God ji, I am sitting in this cybercafé not to chat or to play video games on computer but to write you this letter, a letter that I had been planning to write you for a long time but couldn't do because of the linguistic and postal reasons. I might have further overdue writing this but then I realized that the time had come to take the most important decision of my life and I couldn't wait any longer to write this last letter of my life.

After I got the self-enlightenment to write to you, I was stopped on my way by many letter-blocks. The first and the biggest of those was the language. God ji, this world is full of so many languages that I was confused whether to write you in English, Hindi, Sanskrit, German, Chinese, Arabic or my mother tongue, Punjabi. First, I thought of going by what bulk of this Earth speaks which is Chinese but then I realized that I did not know this language. Then for the same reason I discarded Hindu Temples' language Sanskrit, beautiful *gora's* mother tongue German and panjpeer wale *baba ji's* Arabic.

Nothing is hidden from you, God ji. You know very well that even in this twenty-first century; we, the people of Punjab, consult old people whenever we are refused by our brain's intelligence to figure out a solution for ourselves. I still remember the old days of school fights, when Sukhwinder alias Bhund hit my ass with his hockey stick and there was blood all over my ass. My young school madam went to my old principal ji who in turn consulted our very old village sarpanch ji to figure out what to do. God ji, you know that village sarpanch's in those days were very serious types so our sarpanch Sardar Jarnail Singh ji called for a special session of panchayat to resolve the issue. Normally, we the kids of Dangar Khera were not allowed to go to panchayat because all the village mummy ji's including my mummy late Harmeet Kaur ji thought that it could spoil our character as people in panchayat smoked *beedi*, drank *desi daru* and talked dirty about Hindi and Punjabi films' aunty ji's. However, since it was my case and for a foolproof verdict my ass was to be presented before the five members of panchayat, I went to a panchayat session for the first time.

Even now I feel shamefully aroused that my ass was presented before that panchayat crowd who was smoking, drinking and 'talking dirty about aunties' and to this day, I feel angry with my old principal ji for going to the village sarpanch ji. When all the panchayat members were through with their smoking, drinking and dirty talking, our sarpanch ji called me on the raised platform under peepal tree and very lovingly said:

"You have hidden your ass with so much dirt that we can't study it properly. Please tell us if Bhund hit only on outside or he inserted the stick inside also?"

I did not understand his question but everyone else laughed which made me realize that he had made fun of me and I ran away from the panchayat without answering and without waiting for the judgment. I got so angry that I even decided not to go to sarpanch ji's funeral in case he died before me.

God ji, since I had that experience with sarpanch ji, I did not consult him for the lingual problem of this letter, rather I went to the most educated uncle ji of my village - 'The Father' of the Rock Church. God ji, I don't know why he is called Father without even fulfilling the basic principle of fatherhood which is to reproduce kids but still I respect him very much. Unlike others in my village, he is very hygienic, shaved, polite and non-abusive but the problem is that I don't understand his English as he has a very different style of English. He says, 'you' as thou, 'shall' as shalt and has such funny names for many other words. He told me that I should not even dream of writing to you because 'You' are a very serious business and no one should take your name in vain.

So God ji, not being able to get my answer, I started consulting my intelligent friends and the best advice came from Jagga who suggested that I use technology to conquer my question. God ji, Jagga was my enemy till two years back but then he helped me a lot when I was in Vancouver and thus recovered my friendship. During my Canadian days, he used to keep this café open till late night and sometimes even switched on the generator for my mummy ji, my papa ji and my elder sister to chat with me. God ji, I didn't tell anyone but I chatted a lot with other people when I was in Canada. I am feeling shy to admit that I made three chat girlfriends – 'Smarthotpanty', 'Sexsexybabes' and 'Imnaughty'. While first two were just my normal girlfriends, I fell in love with Imnaughty because she had a computer camera and I used to look into her eyes through that camera. She was a Chinese looking girl from Philippines and never made fun of me or my name. After three months of chatting we decided to get married but then she told me that she could not become Sikh. I was heartbroken because I knew that my papa ji and mummy ji would never agree for my marriage to a Chinese looking non-Sikh girl. Unable to get married, I stopped chatting with her. Caught in grief, I cried a lot at nights for many weeks but that's history and now I am very stable.

After that breakup, I had a small affair with 'Mad_about_sucking' but I left her as she never chatted properly. She had a craze for undressing. Every time after saying, 'Hello', she used to type the same thing "Wanna see me naked, click *http://www.mad_about_sucking.com."*

God ji, these are no more the historic times of our naked monkey ancestors, so how can a girl be always naked? I realized she was not my type; I am naked only when I take bath and that too wearing my *'kachhaihra'* the underwear and I want to make friends only with those who are like me.

So God ji, on Jagga's advice, I decided to chat with religious people from other countries to know your language. Every day, for one full week I used to enter a chat room 'Let's contact God' and chatted with your loved ones. God ji, you don't have an idea how many people in this world want to get in touch with you and when I asked them my doubt, most of them recommended Hebrew, Portuguese and Italian to get in touch with you but in my village I don't have teachers to teach all those. Finally, I was left with no option but to ask my sister, Cute Kaur. God ji, Cute is very intelligent but very *muhphat*. I tell her my problems only when no one else is able to help me. She always offers me the perfect solution but the problem is that whatever I tell her, she forwards that to the entire village. It is for this reason that when I had my breakup with 'Imnaughty', I did not ask her for help.

People say that she behaves like this because she was born on 15th August and since everyone from Prime Minister ji to sarpanch ji lectures on that day, she got that habit in her tongue. God ji, it's also for her birth date that I am very much angry with her because she always has a holiday on her birthday. In good, young, ignorant days when both of us were kids and I did not know the meaning of my name, my mummy ji used to celebrate 'happy birthdays' of both of us on Cute's birthday because of the holiday.

God ji, on our happy birthdays we used to have an *anand path* in the morning followed by *langar* in this very home where all my friends, Jarnail, Ganpat, Sukhwinder and many others used to come and then Cute and I used to blow out the candles and cut cake.

My mummy ji was very practical and had fixed our turns. One year I blew out candles while Cute cut the cake and next year it used to be reverse. God ji, unlike Canada, people in my village are very *'desi'* so they used to eat cake and langar but never gifted us anything. Only once in my life I got a gift, when my mama Sardar Kultar Singh ji, who lived in Canada, was in India on my birthday. He gifted me a pink colored toothbrush.

So God ji, I went to Cute's married home early today evening. As usual, she was in the kitchen boiling milk for my nephew, Laali while my brother-in-law Ganinder alias Giani was watching TV. God ji, Cute got married when I was just twenty and she has one son from her husband.

"*Sat sri akal*, Giani ji. Thanks to *Waheguru* that you are fit and fine, how are others?"

"Hello ji, hello ji, good to see you, so when are you getting married?"

"Giani ji, I beg you to talk something else. I don't want to get married as I have some other plan."

"What plan? Some love-shuv? Or like those *goras* in Canada you have started liking men, *ha ha ha*. *Oye* Cute, did you hear what your brother said?"

"I can't tell the plan now. By the way where is Laali?" I asked about Laali to stop the discussion of my marriage and it worked.

"He has gone to get the video CD of our favorite movie 'Mard'. We will watch it for the ninety-sixth time today."

I wanted to talk to him more about 'Mard' as that was my favorite movie but then I remembered the purpose of my visit so I finished that discussion and went straight to the kitchen.

"*Sat sri akal*, Cute. I want to talk to you about something very important."

"*Oye*, if you wanted to talk to me something important then you could have called me on my mobile. Don't you have my stylish phone number?"

"I have your number as you have given that to me lacs of times, why don't you get it printed on your forehead?"

"I keep telling you my number as you never store it in your mobile. Moreover, you have never ever called me so how do I know that you remember my number?"

"But I think I called you many times."

"Then tell me what my hello tune is?"

Struck by a lightening tough question, I thought of turning aggressive. "Actually, you talk a lot and my expensive recharge card would finish in a single day if I call you."

"Ok ji, you and your cheap excuses. Stop all this and tell me what do you want to talk about? Before that, eat some leftover lunch. I had a feeling that you would come today so I kept some butter chicken in the fridge."

"I will have that later, first you need to help me."

"Tell me ji."

"First, promise me that you will not broadcast it to anyone."

"Ok, promise. I will not tell it to anyone except Kirtan ji, Nandi Aunty, Manpreet, Teesha and if your question is not too garbage, then papa ji and Giani ji also."

"But why can't you just keep your mouth shut?"

"Because I am not like you, I tell everything to Giani ji, papa ji and Kirtan ji."

"Ok but why your neighbors Nandi Aunty and others?"

"Because they are not just my neighbors! Unlike you, they call me regularly on my Nokia 1100."

I did not want to get into the discussion of her beautiful Nokia again so I went straight to the point:

"I want to write a letter to God ji but I don't know which language to write in?"

"Which God ji, you mean papa ji, masar ji or mama ji?"

"No. God ji means God ji, the one we worship in Gurudwara sahib."

"Ohho! You have never cared to write a letter to me, not even one word and now you want to write to God ji? Please don't waste my time on all this, I have to iron clothes."

"Cute, why don't you understand, it's very important."

"And I am not important? Anyway, tell me one thing; even if I tell you the language, what will you write?"

"I will write about my plan and the reasons for the same."

"Oh, so you have some plan-*shlan*. Can I know what it is?"

"No, it is personal."

"Ok but first tell me how you will send the letter. Do you have God ji's address?"

"First, let me write it and then I will think how to send it. Maybe, I will dispatch it via computer email."

"Oh! I forgot that you are very hi-fi. I wish I had also gone to Canada, at least I would have never returned as a failed school kid like you."

She knew that her remarks were making my heart vomit so she continued, "But will God ji understand your handwriting which even your teachers never understood? I still remember your sir ji's and madam ji's always complaining to mummy ji that you would become a doctor because of your handwriting."

"Cute, please don't tell me all that and remember I am not an illiterate like you, I will type it on Jagga's computer."

"Shut up! I am an M.A. in Punjabi. In college, I used computer for two hours once. I am not a donkey like you! If you are going to type your letter on Jagga's computer then type it in the language that's available. Can you type in any other language except English on his computer?"

"Oh! Thank you very much. At last I received my answer."

I was happy. I did not want to talk anymore to anyone in that uncivilized family. I rushed out as soon as I got what I was looking for.

"Sat sri akal , Cute and Giani ji. Tata! I am leaving. I am in a hurry."

"But, your butter chicken?"

"Pack it quickly. I will have it at Jagga's café as I am going there to type my letter."

Even after the problem of the language got solved, there was no end to my doubts as I was unconfirmed about your address. On my way to Jagga's café, I remembered what Gunjeet Madam had once told us in class 3rd A, "*Bachho* when we die, we all go to *Waheguru.*"

Cybercafé - Day II

My Plan

'I want to commit suicide.' God ji, I laid the foundation stone of this plan the day I got to know the meaning of my name and there has been no looking back after that.

That day is still fresh in my memory. It was a very depressing day, like all the other days of that uneventful August of 1990. It was three days after my candle blowing and Cute's cake cutting ceremony and we had full day school and quarter day electricity only for four days in that month.

God ji, I do not know about your heaven but in our state, everything is centred around electricity timings. Starting from the birth of the kids, marriage *muhurats* to death ceremonies - everything is planned based on the inputs from the electricity department and not the priests or *pathis*. People in the electricity board have so much power that they molest 'we the public' at every possible opportunity.

God ji, a lot has changed with time in last twelve years in my village and like all other businesses, Electricity Department too has become very professional and organized. These days our young Lineman Bhatti's old aged wife manages most of the bribery stuff. There are no negotiations and the prices are fixed. God ji, please do not think that the situation is this bad every time, because thrice in every five years at the time of panchayat, assembly and parliament elections we get fifteen hours of electricity and the best part is that we don't even pay bills during those days.

I read it in a special 'Health pullout' of Punjab Kesari that the biggest benefit of elections is for business houses as the sales of condoms and beers go up significantly because of regular electricity during those times.

God ji, other than beer and condom sales, there is one more benefit of elections and that is the chance of sighting big leaders in my small erstwhile school. Not only the regular MLAs and MPs but my school also had the good fortune of having our late Prime Minister, Rajiv Gandhi ji visiting us during one election campaign. I clearly remember his visit. In those days I was a young, handsome, robust man studying in second standard. I was in second standard because I had passed my first standard examination a year before with very good marks. God ji, I am a very intelligent person. I never studied all day long like Cute and still I was always among the toppers with consistent score of more than thirty-three percent marks in all my classes. That was the reason my mummy ji always dreamt of me becoming a Doctor or a Deputy Commissioner but I always thought of becoming the 'Father of Punjab'. With such a good academic record, why waste my aptitude by just being a Doctor or a Deputy Commissioner, especially when there was a huge opportunity available. We have Father of India, Mr. Bapu Gandhi ji but no Father of Punjab. I always wondered why we don't have Father of Punjab and I asked that question to all my teachers also but no one except Gunjeet Madam could realistically answer my question. She told me that we don't have Father of Punjab because our state is a free state. If we ever become slave of some kingdom and then if someone sacrifices his life for our independence like Mr. Bapu Gandhi ji did, then that person could become the Father of the state.

God ji, Rajiv Gandhi ji had to address a rally in Nehru Stadium adjacent to our school. So, he opted to land at the hockey ground of Government Middle School, Dangar Khera in the hot afternoon sun. That was the first time when I saw a helicopter and a Prime Minister. Rajiv ji came, spoke to a few old uncles for some seconds and while leaving, asked us what we wanted from him. One of the girls standing in the front row said that she wanted more holidays, which he promised that he would try. Along with being fair-skinned and smart, he was also a man of words and kept his promise even after his death. Panchayat elections got introduced after his death in 1992 because of which we have additional number of holidays every few years and our Social Sciences madam told us that it all became possible because of the efforts of Rajiv Gandhi ji. Seeing Prime Minister ji in the stadium that evening, I decided that I will also make a stadium, in my mummy's and papa ji's name and then address a rally in Sardar Natha Singh Stadium wearing a white *kurta - pyjama*.

God ji, coming back to that depressing day; I got crowded as soon as I entered the school. There were a lot of unknown youngsters gathered at the school entrance shouting some slogans. Those youngsters shouting slogans outside our school were neither from our village nor from any other village but from some big city. Most of those youngsters shouting slogans outside our school were graduates as they were talking in Hindi and not Punjabi. A few of them sounded like graduates with distinction also as they were speaking broken English. One of them, a short, slim and long- haired boy asked all of us to assemble in the prayer ground. God ji, you would know him as he was your son or maybe you do not know him, as you have so many sons.

All of us assembled in the prayer ground in the format taught to us by Bihari Lal Sir. Bihari Sir was our

NCC and PT sir and he had taught us the art of occasional queuing - how to stand in queues depending on the occasion. On 15th August and 26th January parade, we were supposed to stand in queues of three; in morning prayers we used to stand in queues of four and for nails inspection we were desired to be in a single file. Your son was very patriotic as he changed our queue pattern from four to three. We were not able to understand what was going on as all our teachers were standing on the border of the ground and your son and his friends were in the middle. For a change there was silence in the prayer ground. Your son was talking to his friends and we were clueless about what to do next. We all asked our class monitor, Mota, in whispering tones on the next course of action and he asked us to chorus some prayer to impress your son.

"Where the mind is without fear and the head is held high, where the knowledge is free and…"

"Stop it!" your son shouted.

I did not understand his attitude. On one hand, he loved you so much that he had written 'I am the son of God' in Punjabi on his T-shirt and on the other, he was not letting us pray to you. Maybe he turned offensive because his father's name was being dragged. It was not his fault but all the independent kids think like that. Even I hate it a lot when people take my papa ji's name while discussing about me. It does not mean that I don't respect him; rather I respect him a lot but to be honest with you, I don't think he has done much for me. Once while teaching us about Aurangzeb, Gunjeet Madam had told us that he was a bad man because he put his father in house arrest in one of the rooms on the first floor facing the Taj Mahal but I don't think he was that bad. If one has a useless father who, being a king, is not bothered about running the kingdom but spends twenty years in creating a structure in his wife's memory then what would the frustrated prince do? Given a chance, I would also lock my papa ji in the storeroom at the first floor of our house facing 'Nathhu Kirana Shop'. Not only my papa ji but I would have locked all the useless papas on the first floor of their respective houses had I become the 'Father of Punjab'.

"All of you need to help us," your son shouted and that too in English.

Your son was really behaving like East India Company but that was not his fault. How could he know that English was taught in our school only from fourth standard onwards? I had started learning English that year itself and even after six months in fourth standard I could understand only three words of his, 'of', 'you' and 'to' but as he did not tell the spelling so I thought those to be 'off' 'u' and 'two'. My classmate Ginni, who was standing next to me, was very intelligent in English because his one *bua* and two *chachas* were in England and he was taking extra tuitions in English too. I never took tuitions because I was afraid that it would harm my career. Nobody would accept me as the 'Father of Punjab' if they knew that I took tuitions in school. Everyone would have asked, "Why does one need tuitions to become a father?"

I asked Ginni as to what your son meant. He replied, "I have understood 'off', 'you', 'two', and 'us'. I think he means that two of us should go and switch off fans and lights in all the classes."

"Who two?"

"He did not mention any names because he does not know anyone. I think both of us should go, maybe he will give us some prize for that."

"But why us, let someone from the senior classes go."

"They will not go because no one other than two of us understood what he said. Let us not spoil the reputation of our school by giving him an impression that no one understood his English."

Ginni and I stepped out and he shouted, "I and he, ji."

He was really very good in English, I thought. He did not stop there but continued, "I and he fan off class ji."

This was the first time in the history of Dangar Khera that someone spoke one full original sentence in English and that too in front of the entire school. All the students started clapping and both of us ran towards the classrooms. Ginni was too good. He was our hero that day.

God ji, there were eight classrooms, one bathroom, one staff room, one library-cum-sports-cum-music-cum-art room, one principal's room and one canteen in our school.

Ginni and I were very happy. He was happy because he had become the hero of the school and I was happy because he chose me as his partner. We were sure that by doing what we were doing, we had guaranteed a place for ourselves in the school's history books; that all those standing in the hockey ground were in their hearts feeling like the dust of our feet.

First, we went to our classroom 4th A and found that the fans and the bulbs were already off. We went to other classrooms and it was the same everywhere. Then we understood how ignorant we had been. Every morning the bulbs and fans were switched on by the students on entering the class but since no one had entered the classrooms that day, all the fans and bulbs were off. Hence, we decided to spend some time in 1st B before returning so as to give an impression that we were really switching off the fans and bulbs or all the students would have laughed at us. Since we needed to do something in that classroom to murder the time, we started searching all the benches but did not find anything of our interest.

We came back to the prayer ground expecting a heroes' welcome but the assembly was over by then. All the students had changed their positions from standing to sitting, in circular groups of seven to eight each, the way girls used to sit during recess. Your son and his friends were distributing some stationery to all the groups. No one paid any attention to us. We went to the group where Jagga, Jarnail and Ganpat were sitting. They asked us to move to some other group, as they did not want any trouble because of us. We went to Mota and he also did not want to talk to us.

We felt completely helpless and were unable to understand why everyone was avoiding us. Then I saw Cute sitting with her friends.

"What happened, nobody is talking to us?"

"What are you doing here? Go to your classmates."

"But no one is talking to us."

"Because Raman *bhapa* is angry with both of you."

"Who is Raman?"

"The leader of those pigeons." she indicated towards your son.

"But, why is he angry with us?"

"Because you ran away from the assembly when he was speech-ing. He got mad and asked about both of you. Anyway, no one told him anything but now go, hide and don't show him your face."

I rushed back to my class group and sat with my back facing the Sun ji. I had not even settled when that one of your son's friends came and gave our group a set of two chart papers, two sketch pens and one sheet having a handwritten slogan to copy on the chart papers.

Unable to control his confusion, Ganpat asked, "What do we do with these charts and sketch pens?"

The ever attentive Jagga replied "He has asked us to copy this English slogan and draw some cartoons on these chart papers."

"But why same slogan on both the charts?"

"No idea, I don't understand all this. *Oye* Ginni, since you understand English, why don't you become our group leader and dictate us what to do?"

"I don't want to become the leader of people like you, who don't even understand English."

Before our group could further listen to his influential logic, I shouted, "Ginni, please be our leader because if we are not able to finish this work then how will we go and play cricket?"

Cricket was Ginni's weakness. Though, he was a bad cricketer but he used to still play it all the time. He did not play it out of his liking for the game but because he had to go to England one day and he thought that girls there liked cricket players more than marble players.

"I will take this responsibility only on one condition. In today's match, I will be opening batsman and nobody will run me out."

We had no option as none of us even had a tiny fraction of his English skills so we all nodded in agreement.

"Ok, let us start. Ganpat, you go and fill my water bottle."

Ginni was an outstandingly foresighted leader. He was not going to use the sketch pens but water colors.

Half impressed, half jealous I asked, "Ginni, are you carrying the water colors?"

"For what?"

"For coloring these chart papers. That's why you are asking for water, right?"

"No. How stupid of you! I need water to wet this handwritten sheet of paper. None of you know what is written on this and I am sure you can't properly copy it also, so we will put water on this. In the end, we would steal someone else's chart paper and submit that. No one would be able to catch us as cross checking with the wet paper would not be possible."

"But what will we do with this chart and these sketch pens?"

"We will make some great paintings on these, which we will send to Jhujhar. My mama ji told me that paintings sell for a huge price in England, so much so that some people don't do farming or any government job but just make paintings and survive on those."

"But what do we paint? We know nothing except how to make Sun ji, Moon, hut, river, tree and mountain, which we learnt in our drawing class."

"No problem, that's more than enough. We have two chart papers. Three of you will make Sun, Moon and hut on one chart and three of us including me, will make river, trees and mountain on the other one. Ganpat will go and get water."

I wanted to be in Ginni's group as I was good in making river, trees and mountain but sadly I was put in the other group.

With the chart beneath my knees and sketch pen in my hand, I started making the most beautiful Sun ji, Moon and hut of my life. My group members Jarnail and Bhupinder were very happy to have an artist like me in their group and they did not interfere much. I assigned Jarnail the job of making border with the pencil and Bhupinder to press the loose end of the chart paper with his hands. I made a big hut in the centre with a small door and two big windows, a small Sun ji on the left and a big Moon on the right. All were in my favorite color, blue. Thankfully, that was the only sketch pen I had or I would have got unnecessarily confused. In order to differentiate between Sun ji and Moon, I made twenty-four small lines projecting out of the Sun ji. I completed my painting in eighteen minutes and then took five minutes to sign my name on the roof of the hut with 18/08/1990 written under it.

As soon as we finished, Ginni ran away and returned in no time, with another chart paper. He had stolen it from some girls group and as usual, they had drawn sketches of a lot of vegetables and utensils alongside the slogan. We started reading their chart;

'We don't want Mandal Commission, we don't want reservation; all we want is politicians working to make us a happy and progressive nation' with Mandal Commission written inside a frying pan, reservation in a water jug, nation on a *tawa*, all the 'i' in the form of carrots, 's' in the form of beans and 'o' as tomatoes and potatoes.

None of us understood what that slogan meant and none of us except Jagga wanted to understand.

"What does this mean?"

"I also don't know but if you look around, two words are common in all the posters, 'Mandal' and 'Reservation'."

While all of us were busy making our paintings, Ganpat after getting the water had been looking around. All of us started staring at Ginni for him to throw some light on those two words and he did not disappoint us.

"I have read 'reservation' on the ticket counter at the railway station and 'mandal' on the godown in *anaj mandi*. Haven't you ever noticed?"

Though all of us had been to the *anaj mandi* many a time to play cricket but it was only Ginni who had noticed the word 'mandal' written on the godown. Ginni continued his knowledge-rain with a very serious and depressing face, "The word mandal means city and reservation means something related to train tickets. I am sure these slogans mean that the train tickets should be given to city people only."

We all turned red. It was not that we traveled a lot by train. Our village was self sufficient for all the important needs but for certain unimportant requirements like medicines and outdoor clothes we used to go to the nearest metropolitan, Abohar and that too in bus.

"I will not let this happen. If needed, I will fight like Mr. Bapu Gandhi ji, indulge in hunger strikes and struggle till my last breath to ensure that train tickets are there for us villagers also."

Though I was showing my anger to others but deep down I was happy that finally I had a cause to fight which could help me in becoming the Father of Punjab. I would visit all the villages like Mr. Bapu ji did and convince the people to oppose any move by city people to control the trains. I would also start a movement 'City People, Quit Punjab.'

Till then, I had always thought trains to be just a mode of transportation, but that day, I realized that they could become the mode of my salvation also.

"I am not bothered about all this as I will leave this village to settle in England very soon, where I will have big trains with a lot of seats without any worry. However, you are my friend so I can bunk school and go with you for normal strike but not a hunger strike. I can never leave my food."

Taking a cue from Ginni, Jarnail said, "I too can't remain hungry for more than two hours. By the way, thank you for reminding me about food." He took out his lunch box and started eating.

"Though I would have liked to join you in the hunger strike but my dadi ji is already angry at me for being so thin. Still, if you insist then I can leave water, onion and tomato and that too for one or two days but I can't leave milk, butter, *parantha*, chicken, *chana-bathura*, *samosa* and *aloo tikki*." 3 feet 10 inches and 59kg Ganpat was at his diplomatic best. He started eating too.

Seeing both of them, others in our group also started eating, and seeing others in our group, the neighboring groups started eating and in no time, all the students left their chart papers and started having lunch at 08.30 A.M. in the morning. Some of them even converted their chart papers to paper plates and put *paranthas* and vegetables on those.

"*Paaji*, what are these complicated slogans? What do they mean?"

Puppi from standard 3rd B asked his question so loudly to one of your son's friends that entire school turned silent and started eyeing him. Puppi was very famous in our school. He was very mature as he was gifted with a small goat like beard in standard 2nd B itself. He was my classmate in standard 1st A. He failed miserably for two years while I passed with super-duper marks and became his senior. In fact, not only me but many of my school seniors also had been his classmates from time to time.

Without answering Puppi's question, your son's friends blew a whistle, a whistle sounding similar to the PT sir's morning whistle. We all stood up and started assembling in queues.

"One of you asked the meaning of these slogans," this time your son was speaking in Hindi. He continued, "Did anyone understand the meaning of these?"

Most of the students of my class looked at Ginni and a few looked at me too. I did not understand why your son was asking us the meaning. Maybe, he also did not know what those slogans meant.

"So, no one here has the basic knowledge of English to understand even this much. Shame on you!"

Ginni, the one with most of his relatives in England could not accept someone shaming his English knowledge. He shouted in English,

"You many train tickets - Jalandhar, Ludhiana, Patiala, Amritsar, Chandigarh. We train tickets one Dangar Khera. No chart papers, no slogans, we *sirf* tickets."

Not only his tongue but also his hands were in action. While speaking he tore off the poster, which he had stolen from the group of girls.

"What train tickets? What Jalandhar, Chandigarh, Delhi?"

Ginni had never mentioned Delhi; your son had turned confused and lost his mental balance. He was speaking in Hindi in response to Ginni's English. Now I was sure that he did not know English and when faced with a smart English speaker like Ginni, he had completely gone mad. However, Ginni did not lose confidence and with a red face, continued in English, "We Dangar Khera happy. We children happy game cricket and food *parantha*, uncles happy water and *daru*, aunties happy talk. Children, uncles, aunties, mummy jis, papa jis, *masi jis, bua jis* happy. Each happy. You make we unhappy. You go back. Train zindabad, Station zindabad."

"Train zindabad, Station zindabad," our class shouted with him.

"Train zindabad, Station zindabad," our entire school shouted, not once, not twice but till your son shouted back.

"Shut up!"

But neither Ginni nor we stopped.

"Bole so Nihal." Pummi came running towards our class and started beating one of your son's friend. Unable to resist that lucrative opportunity a lot of other students also jumped on him.

"Train zindabad, Station zindabad," someone in the group shouted and again the entire school joined the chorus.

Your son and his other friends came rushing but they were too late. By the time they reached and figured out how to save their friend, we had done the desired, requisite damage. Their friend was bleeding from the nose, chin and forehead; his shirt's right arm was torn and his spectacles were broken. Our PT sir also reached the crime spot.

"Who started all this?" your son angrily asked.

Everyone in unison pointed towards his injured friend and that made him even angrier.

"We are here to help you out and you are beating us!"

"What help? You want to stop the train tickets to our village."

Both your son and Ganpat were talking in Hindi.

"Who told you that we are here to stop train tickets?"

"That's what these slogans mean."

"Oh my God!"

"This is crazy! What a shit place we have come to!" the injured friend yelled in English while getting up.

"Shit means *tatti*, he is calling us *tatti*." Ginni had learnt that word from Jhujhar. On hearing that, all of us attacked the injured friend one more time.

Another whistle and this time, it was a familiar one. PT sir standing next to us whistled so loudly that we had no option but to leave everything and stand in queues again.

"Sons of donkeys, behave properly. No one will fight now."

PT sir was very angry. 'Sons of donkeys' was his expression of extreme anger and disgust beyond which his cane used to overtake his words.

"All of you keep quiet and listen to what your elder brothers have to say."

"I don't know why you people are behaving like this, there seems to be some misunderstanding," your son was now speaking in full-blooded Punjabi. God ji, I do not understand what kind of education they have in the cities. In a span of an hour, your son had transformed from being a graduate with distinction to a matriculate villager.

"*Veer ji, Sat sri akal.* I am Puppi Singh, son of Sardar Yograj Sandhu and Sardarni Harwant Kaur of village, Nihal Khera. All of us are very upset with you because you played with our hearts today. Let me tell you that we may be villagers but we are actually very smart. You come to our school, you spoil our study time and you ask us to write so much in English. We don't know your name, your father's name or your city and we still did so much for you but in return you want to stop the sales of train tickets to us."

There was no one in our school who was as mature and brave as Puppi. No fear, no hesitation, no confusion and he clearly spoke what all of us had in our minds.

While I was introspecting what all Puppi had said, some students shouted, "*Puppi bai hero hai, Shehri munde zero hai.*"

Another whistle, another 'sons of donkeys' and we all turned quiet.

"You are like our younger brothers. Why would we play with your hearts or stop the sales of train tickets? We are not from Railways but from Sant Singh College, Abohar and we are here to ask for your help."

I immediately became attentive and started respecting your son. He was from my dream college. There was only one college 'Sant Singh College' in Abohar and all of us wanted to study there.

Ganpat whispered, "What help can we be of?"

Jarnail replied in whisper, "Maybe they need something which we have but they don't have."

"I will tell my Papa ji to make sarpanch ji aware about this conspiracy."

"Entire village knows that even your mummy ji does not listen to your papa ji so why would sarpanch ji listen to him?"

"Veer ji, what help do you need? I can arrange *lassi* while others can arrange milk and lunch for you, or we can teach you cricket and *bhangra*. I don't think we can help you in any other way," Puppi moved both his hands up in *balle balle* action of *bhangra* while talking in a melodious and relieved tone this time.

"We don't need your help for all these things but we need your help to fight the government."

"*Veer ji*, if you need help to fight someone then you have come to the right place, we are always ready to fight anyone, anytime. Tell us how many hockeys, bats and *gandaseys*, do you need?"

"We don't need all those dangerous weapons but we want you to bunk your school for a few days, be on the roads and help us in generating public opinion against the policies of the government," your son was unnecessarily speaking in a loud tone. Maybe to let his in-charge in Abohar hear what he was saying so that he could get full marks for his efforts. However, I was still not sure about their dispatcher so I asked Jarnail, "Who has sent them to our village?"

"Pakistan army!" came the prompt reply.

It was not the only instance when I was hearing that. It was an open secret in our village that Pakistan army was responsible for all our problems.

"Papa ji told me that Pakistan army men are not brave and they take the help of children whenever they have to fight enemies," Jarnail's papa ji was a retired honorary Subedar from army and he always had many interesting stories to share about Pakistan army.

"*Veer ji*, who is this Government? What are its policies? I am sorry but in our village, we can't be on the roads because we don't have any road. There are only '*kuchcha* lanes' and fields there."

"Government means Prime Minister V.P. Singh and we are fighting against his policy of reservation which has been recommended by the Mandal Commission. Don't worry about the roads, whenever required we will take you to Abohar in tractors."

I am sure that no one in the assembly ground understood a bit of what your son said but the thought of bunking the classes and going to Abohar on tractors was so exciting that everyone cheerfully clapped and raised their right hands with a loud roar of, "V.P. Singh *zindabad, veer ji zindabad, inqualab zindabad.*"

"*Veer ji*, if you want our tractors then please talk to sarpanch ji. Don't worry about driving. We can do that, papa ji sleep afternoon, daily I tractor."

Ginni, who had been silent for some time, could not control himself anymore. His papa ji had two tractors, Mahindra and HMT - both brand new. My papa ji also had a tractor but it was old, so old that I could not even read the name of the company. Unlike other village children, I learnt driving tractor very late, at the age of nine. All my friends had learnt tractor by then but papa ji being a useless papa did not teach me that. I requested, pleaded and begged but even then, he did not relent. Left with no option, I warned him of pouring red-chili on his favorite buffalo's ass, knowing fully well that he would surely be blackmailed by that and it worked.

God ji, learning tractor is very enigmatic - quite easy for a villager but very difficult for an urbanite because tractors are about mindset and urbanites have a problem with that. For example; what would an urbanite call someone, who has one leg much shorter than the other, who farts from nose and not ass, who needs someone to churn a big spoon in his mouth to wake him up every morning, who has an unsymmetrical disfigured body and two dumb brains. He would call him irrelevant and ignore him as a useless creation whereas for a villager, it's the description of a tractor. A tractor has unsymmetrical tires, a silencer on its nose, two sets of gears, needs a steel bar to start and has a distorted shape.

Not only Ginni but all of us were also on cloud nine because our *veer ji* was going to help us in realizing the passion of every rural child in Punjab, to drive a tractor from one's village to one's tehsil.

"Thank you, but there is no need for the tractors now, we will arrange those ourselves when the time comes. All we need today is that all of you paste these posters on the village walls. We will tell you the meaning of these posters so that you can explain the same to your fellow villagers and this way you will also learn English. Many of these posters are repetitive and we still have some time before the last government bus. I am sure we can finish it in time."

Your son was doing a lot for us even after his friend was beaten. While our papa ji's in collaboration with our mummy ji's had given us birth, you son was the one who was adding meaning to it - bunking school, being on Abohar's roads, driving tractors and now a chance, to master English, in a few hours. In the previous half an hour, that depressing day had become the best day of my school life without me having a clue about what was in store for me next.

Your son and his friends started collecting the posters. Once done, they stood in a line facing us. One of them started acting like a black-board holding one poster at a time in his hands in front of his face and chest, and your son started reading those aloud explaining their meaning to us.

'Schools and Colleges are heaven, but Mandal Commission will make these barren.'

"'Schools' you know, 'colleges' you know, 'heaven' is the best place in the sky, 'but' means *parantu*, 'make' means to do something, 'it' you know and 'barren' is infertile land."

'Bus stops at bus stand, aero plane stops at airport and train stops at railway station. When will our Prime Minister's madness stop and when will he think of something other than Mandal Commission and reservation?'

"Bus you know, 'stop' is to halt, bus stand you know…"

'*Kachuaa-chhaap* kills mosquitoes, spray kills pests; reservation will kill our future before we become birds from eggs in our nests.'

"*Kachuaa-chhaap* you know, 'kill' is to murder, 'spray' you know…"

By then, we realized that we were not that bad in English. We already knew more than half of the words. All of us felt proud about ourselves and we clapped.

Just then, Ganpat shouted at me. "*Oye*, your name is on the poster."

"Who wrote this one? I am sure it's the work of Dheeru. Have some shame, please change this," your son while speaking was laughing loudly and so were his friends.

"No *veer ji*, please don't do this, I will paste this outside my home," I shouted.

How could I let that moment of recognition go away like that? I had waited more than ten years for that day.

"Do you even know its meaning? Ha ha ha."

Your son had really transformed; he was behaving like one of us. He was laughing '*Ha Ha Ha*' loudly like villagers, very much different from the conventional urbane '*He He He.*'

"Yes."

"Oh God! You don't know the basic English like 'A' for Apple, 'B' for Bat and you know this!" He was surprised, confused and worried all at the same time and he could not stop laughing.

"There is no need to be so surprised, all my friends and classmates know this; even my dumb sister knows this."

"Look at this generation, I really need to salute you." With that, he folded his hands in *namaskar* posture and bent completely.

"What's there to laugh, can I not know my name?"

"Name? Whose name?"

"My name, who else." I changed my posture from 'relax' to 'attention' position of NCC. Legs straight, chest out and head firm with pride.

"What's your name?"

"As if you don't know, why don't you ask Dheeru, the one who wrote my name?"

He started reading that poster loudly, "Caste System, Mandal Commission and Reservation, this way our honorable Prime Minister will fuck our nation."

"Yes," I shouted, still in 'attention' position.

"So, what's your name? Mandal?"

"No!"

"Then?"

I cleared my throat, breathed in that dusty air to the count of four and with a voice loud enough to let the entire school hear, said:

"Fuck."

"What?"

"Fuck Singh, Son of both Sardar Makhan Singh ji and Harmeet Kaur ji."

Neither on TV nor in films, neither awake nor in dreams, had I ever seen someone laughing so loudly. Surprisingly your son stopped laughing and asked, "Do you know the meaning of your name?"

Though I knew that my name was adopted from some Canadian God but I did not know its exact meaning, however there was nothing to laugh at it.

"No and I know that even you don't know the meaning of your name, Raman."

"My name is not important but your name is, its meaning is the essence of our life."

I was happy to hear what he was saying; important and essence of life were things like *parantha* and chicken.

Your son came closer to me and in next nineteen seconds described the meaning of my name in super-audible voice. That was the first but not the last time in my life when I wished that I was born deaf. Each of those nineteen seconds were heavier than Mount Everest ji for me. After those nineteen seconds enlightenment, my perspective about others and their perspective about me changed to a level that I made this plan of committing suicide. From that day onwards, I stopped envying people who are rich, powerful or *gora* but started feeling jealous of those who do not know the meaning of their name.

God ji, I know that tomorrow some people might wonder as to why an intelligent, smart, sharp, successful, magnetic, virgin young Punjabi like me committed suicide but I want them to know that I took this decision because after those nineteen seconds my life became my namesake.

"*Behan c***, kutte, saley,*" I shouted at your son and ran away.

Cybercafé - Day III

The Worst Mama Ji Of The World

God ji, now I know for sure how I was born but years ago, had you asked my mummy ji or papa ji, they would have told you that one fine day, they went upstairs on rooftop, prayed to you for a child and I was dropped in their hands from somewhere in the sky. You should not be surprised to hear all this because by now you also know that my papa ji was a liar. Though my mummy ji was a truthful lady but as one bad apple stinks the entire fridge, living with a liar for so many years would have surely affected her too. Since you are God ji and I am not like my papa ji, I must tell you the truth. The truth, a part of which I got to know from my cousin, Sary and the rest from the accidental recall of my pre-childhood memories in my dreams; the truth that I was born and not dropped from the sky; and the truth that I was born because of two people - Mr. Richard Trevithick and Mr. John Walker - the former, for being too slow and the latter, for being too fast. Both of them were Britishers like Jhujhar, intelligent like me and old like Mr. Bapu Gandhi ji. While Mr. Richard was so slow that he could not even ensure his invention 'Heater' reached Punjab's winter-full villages in over two hundred years, Mr. John got his invention 'Whisky' flow like rivers in Punjab in no time.

God ji, Sary is not only intelligent but she has a great sense of information also. Though she has never lived in Punjab and was never ever remotely associated to mummy ji but she still told me the uncensored story of my birth. Maybe, she learnt it in her so- called MBA. She began my birth story by telling me that Punjab's weather is like prostitutes - steaming hot like the Jamaican ones in summer and frigid cold like the Chinese ones in winter. It was on one such night in the winter of 1979 when papa ji and mummy ji laid my foundation stone.

It was 1st of January, a Monday. While temperature during the day was eight degree celsius, it was only one degree celsius in the evening. In all likelihood, it was raining because that's when men drink more alcohol and are super erect. Papa ji came home at seven thirty in the evening and directly went to the kitchen. He was smelling of *desi daru* that his friend Kultar had brewed at home. As soon as mummy ji inhaled him, she shouted, "*Bebey*, take care of your drunkard son or I will break his nose with my *belan*, blind him with my *chimta* and then go back to my *peke* taking my dowry and Cute along."

"Stop shouting and don't call *bebey*."

"Then what do I do with you? Make your pickle or what? I am sure that would also stink like you. *Oye sharabi*, get out of the kitchen right now!"

"First, give me a glass and some *papad*."

"*Hai main mar jawaan*, you are still not full? Have some shame; you have a young daughter and a very young wife at home."

"Harmeetttttttttt," he yelled so loudly that Cute who was sleeping peacefully in the bedroom till then also started crying.

My mummy ji who was not new to this kind of situations understood that he was too drunk to listen to anyone and so, she wanted to teach him a lesson. She gave him an unclean glass and a half- baked *papad*.

"Haramjadi!" and papa ji went to the storeroom on the rooftop.

In exactly twenty-three minutes, papa ji finished the whisky bottle given to him free by Kultar Uncle. Even after finishing his *desi*, papa ji did not come down. He sat on the old bamboo chair with his legs wide open in the doorway of the storeroom enjoying the rain and feeling like an emperor. He did not want to spoil the peace of his drunk, chaotic mind by going down and talking to same old mummy ji who had been with him for so many years.

"Roti is ready. Come down in five minutes if you want to have it or I will feed it to stray dogs."

He obeyed. However, he did not like the food as there was only one *daal*, that too his un-favourite *chana daal* and had a deficit of salt.

"Haramjadi," he again uttered the same word as soon as he finished the dinner and went straight to his bed room, the one and only room in the entire house earmarked for him and his family to sleep.

Mummy ji finished her dinner, cleaned the utensils, heated two glasses of milk and went to the same room. By the time she went, papa ji was lying on the bed in his sando vest and striped *kachhaihra* while Cute was sleeping. She took Cute in her lap and started nipple feeding her.

"I also want to drink milk," papa ji who was in 50% dreams and 50% reality, requested her in his intoxicated tone.

"As if you are still thirsty after having a full bottle of *desi*. Anyway, open your eyes and look at the table, your glass is kept there," mummy ji replied in a firm tone.

"But I want to drink milk the way Cute is drinking."

"*Hai!* Have you donated your entire shame to beggars?"

"It is not my shameless lust but my concern for Cute. I can't see her alone; she needs to have someone to play with."

"*Kutte*, I know you very well," mummy ji smiled and moved Cute from her lap to the *duppata* cum hammock, tied to the two legs of the bed on her side.

Papa ji blew the kerosene lamp off, dragged mummy ji into the quilt, removed his sando vest and *kachhaihra,* and started drinking milk, the way Cute was drinking a few minutes back.

It was raining and lightening outside, and both of them did some shameful things, which led to my birth on the first day of the October of 1979, a day before the happy birthday of the Father of our Nation, Mr. Bapu Gandhi ji.

God ji, in our Punjab, when a boy is born, the major problem is building a consensus on his name. While *dada, dadi, nana, nani* want a name of their choice on emotional grounds claiming that the newborn might be the last boy to be born before they die, other relatives want a name of their liking on mythological grounds giving 'your' example on how you were named by either your *chacha ji, mama ji* or *bua ji* in your different *avatars* without realizing that you had hundreds of births and you could accommodate everyone. Not only the relatives but also the friends of the papa ji and mummy ji want their choices to be considered citing the name of some baba or saint to whom they prayed for their friend's boy. If all this is not chaotic enough, even papa and mummy of the boy have their differences on what name to have. While mummy jis want a name which is good, meaningful and namesake of some great person like Dharmendra, Dara Singh or Navjot Sidhu, papa jis want a name which is long, wild, and exciting like Sher, Shamsher or Babbar Sher. Because of these reasons, most of the boys have hundreds of *kuchcha* names but the schools allow only one *pukka* name and that is a very tough decision.

God ji, I was born in our home; in the only room on the ground floor designated for my father's family. Today morning when I woke up in the same room by the same old wake up call of the same old papa ji, I became emotional and felt the same way I did thirty-one years ago, on the first day of October. I have changed in all these years but the room hasn't. Everything from the disfigured painful cotton mattress that still smells of my childhood urine to the corroded iron almirah with protruding hinges which tear off a few clothes every month, is same except the picture on the wall. The 5"X4" picture of papa ji and mummy ji clicked at Royal Studio, Chandigarh on their honeymoon has been replaced with a garlanded 10"X8" picture of only mummy ji, clicked at our home during Cute's wedding. Had papa ji died along with mummy ji, then I would have garlanded that old picture itself.

By the time I was two days old, I had seen enough of this world to realize that I had only one true friend – 'my penis'. Like me, it was small, soft, delicate and both of us understood each other quite well. I could touch it when I felt lonely, could play with it when I felt bored and could use it to urinate on others when I wanted to get away from them. Other than my penis, everyone else around me was insensitive, predictable, dumb and hungry.

My papa ji was very happy with me during those initial few days as all my visitors literally 'paid' me a visit. I was his goldmine. Whenever someone visited me, he or she would keep either a ten or twenty rupee note on my pillow side. While it did not surprise me to know them worshipping me so much that they gave donations to see me, what surprised me was to see my lazy papa ji rushing to grab those notes. Now that I know him well, I can understand the kind of thoughts going on in his mind at that time - 'With this ten-rupee, the total is thirty now. Cheers! I can buy a quarter of Bagpiper', 'Today's collection is only fifteen rupees, I will have to be satisfied with a *desi* only', 'If I can have one boy child every month, I need not work to earn my drinks', '*Saley*, only five rupees! Have I have fathered a beggar?'

At the age of six days, I heard my first English word 'Hello'. Imagine someone six to seven times taller, twenty times heavier, wearing a suit and a necktie, holding me - a six days old mature child - in his big rough hands and talking in English. Unable to come to terms with that situation, I puked. Without having a clue that my puke would immediately transform that sophisticated English speaking man to a downtrodden Punjabi. "*Oye behan de*, you got only your imported mama to puke on!" His words irritated me further and I even thought of excreting on that imported giant but sadly, there was no pressure in my asshole. I was unhappy but my papa ji was excited as he got a note of Rs.500 from that imported relative, which was more than sufficient for him to bear not just one but also hundreds of my insults.

With my mama ji's arrival, not only me but also our hand pump got upset as the center of our house shifted from that pump to him. The reason was obvious as he had all the three things, which one needs to make others lick one's ass in Punjab - fair wife, English language and bottles of imported whisky and he used all the three very effectively to lay his claim as the grantor of my name.

My papa ji and mama ji had a very agricultural relationship. When my papa ji, after his first wedding, met mama ji for the first time, they struck a friendship at first sight. God ji, when two people become very close friends in Punjab, they give each other not just gifts but something more than that - a nick name. A name, which they think the other person, resembles in entirety. That's how my papa ji started calling him *Jhona* which means rice in Punjabi and mama ji who till then used to call him jija ji named him as *Ganna,* the sugarcane. Strangely, they nick named each other very intelligently despite their low IQ.

God ji, if you think that my mama ji travelled all the way to Dangar Khera to see me then you are wrong beyond correction because he came from Canada just for one reason - 'to show off'. This was the reason of his two weeks visit and he would come every two years with a mindset exactly like that of the previous trips. He had a fixed routine. He would reach Delhi Airport in the early morning hours, board Janta Express at Delhi railway station to reach Bathinda in the evening and once in Bathinda, he would call mummy ji on our p.p. number which was at Lovely Uncle's home located at the end of our lane. Though Lovely ji did not charge anything but anyone who went to receive a call generally carried something for his wife. My mama ji normally used to come in winter so my mummy ji used to take three pieces of *pinni* or four pieces of *burfi* whenever Lovely Uncle's son came running to our place to announce, "Canada wale mama ji called from Bathinda. He will call again in ten minutes."

"Hello, welcome me to India!"

"Bhape ki?"

"Oh! I am sorry, I forgot that my villager sister does not even know fundamental English. Anyway, *Sat sri akal.*"

"Sat sri akal."

"Waheguru."

"Waheguru."

"I don't know why I spend so much of my expensive money on aero plane to come to India every 2-3 years. It's so hot and dusty and then you have bad water here. Your Shammi *bhabhi* fell sick within a few minutes of landing at Delhi's big airport. I had no option but to spend a lot of my expensive money to stay at Grand Look for next two days, where they charge Rs.15 for a plate of *daal* and Re.1 for a *roti.*"

"Who will take care of her in the *hotall*, you come home today and I will make her fit in no time."

"It's not *hotall* but *hotel.* Anyway, you neither have a TV nor a good radio at your small home. How will you cure her without providing her proper entertainment?"

"Shammi is no *mem*. She was born and brought up in Ghubaya, which is more backward than Dangar Khera. She did not even have a sense to plait her hair when she got married and look at her now. Papa ji and I advised you so many times not to marry her but her white color had blinded a stupid like you beyond imagination to pay heed to our advices."

"Harmeet, do you want me to meet you or shall I return to Canada from here itself?"

"Hai hai, look at the way you are talking. There was a time when you never stepped out of the home without asking me and look at you now. I am sure your wife must have taught you all this."

"Enough! Say my *Sat sri akal* to Ganna, I will see him in two days."

After spending two days in Grand Look, mama ji used to come to the village by the 2 P.M. bus and papa ji used to collect him from the bus stand. After that, it used to be the same story every day for next ten days. Both mama ji and mami ji spent the entire time eating, sleeping and comparing Canada to our village except that mama ji used to drink also. Every evening, he and papa ji along with a few important parasitic villagers from Punjab Police, Electricity Board, local State Bank branch and panchayat used to meet on our terrace to drink some imported whisky from a black or red colored bottle. While mama ji's entire focus used to be talking and boasting about his Canadian life, others in the group focused on finishing their glasses as quickly as possible and spoke a few monosyllables of surprise or small questions in between to be a part of the discussion.

"I feel good to offer such an expensive whisky of ten dollars to you beasts because I earn a lot. President of Amrikka also drinks this whisky."

"Oh!"

"Does he drink with soda or water?"

"With *Amritsari papad* or banana?"

"You dickheads! He is the President of Amrikka! Why would he eat *papad?*"

"Really!"

"That's not a big deal! Even our sarpanch ji takes whisky with *papad*."

"Dickheads, President of Amrikka is much more expensive than sarpanch of Dangar Khera."

"Ah!"

"Jhona ji, what is this *angreji* word that you keep speaking again and again, Dikkhad?"

"I think it means brothers."

"No, I know English, it means *darubaaj*, one who drinks a lot. Jhona ji, this is not good. First, you fill us with whisky and then, call us drunkard."

"Assholes, I did not say drunkard, I said dickhead, it means stupid."

"Oh!"

"Really!"

"Now, what is this new *angreji* word, Ashool? Jhona ji, please don't use such difficult *angreji* especially when we are dikkhad."

"*Ha ha ha!*"

"I know English, It's not *angrjei* but Hindi word, ashool means principle in *angreji*."

"Jhona ji, how can you forget so quickly? I told you yesterday itself that I am a Sub-Inspector and not a principal, anyway thank you very much for calling me a principal. When I met Preeto for the first time on her *Kotakpura wali* sister's wedding, even she thought that I was a headmaster."

"*Oye behan de!* Stop your record of Preeto and I did not say Principal, asshole means *gaandu*."

"*Acchha!*"

"Leave all that and see this watch. This is a computer watch. No hands and no need to screw it every morning. This watch also has a bulb inside it and if I press this button, it shows the date too."

"This is really hi-fi, it must be very expensive." Finally, papa ji used to compliment on that one thing, which he wanted as a gift.

Mama ji used to think for some time and then depending on what his empty brain would say, he would either ignore papa ji or stand up and speak so loudly to ensure that it was audible to distant neighbors also.

"Ganna, nothing is dearer than you. Though it takes many years for a villager like you to earn what you need to afford this kind of watch, I will still gift it to you."

"Show me, show me!"

"I also want to see!"

"Give it in my hand."

Most of the times their evenings used to end with these discussions but on a few days, especially during the fag end of mama ji's trip when because of the scarcity of imported whisky, they drank leftover imported whisky mixed with *desi* whisky, they spoke a lot of bad stuff about white aunties of Canada; the way old people spoke about village aunties in the panchayat. I never understood what exactly they talked but I knew for sure that they chatted dirty, because on those few days, mummy ji used to force us to get into bed and cover our ears with quilt. It was during one of those evenings that my name was decided.

The day of my nomenclature was very long. Mummy ji woke me up very early in the morning. It had been just a few peaceful moments after I woke up that mummy ji got into action. She started applying ghee, first on my hair and then on my body. I knew that it was the time for me to have milk, not for drinking but for bathing. It was my thirteenth day in this world and by then, I had started understanding different actions of mummy ji. Massaging me meant time for bath, taking me in lap meant feeding time and whispering *sheee sheee sheee* was an indication to urinate. Unlike these actions which I hated, there were a few of her gestures which I liked - when she tickled my stomach or put her finger in my fist. There was no hidden meaning attached to those actions and that's why I liked those. Once done with massage, mummy ji washed my entire body with our buffalo's milk which did not smell bad that day, rather it did not smell at all because I had not been able to smell anything since previous evening as I had caught cold.

For a change, mummy ji dressed me in brand new clothes. I could not understand what was happening. Once I was ready, mummy ji handed me over to papa ji, who in turn put me on mama ji's lap.

"*Waheguru, waheguru…*," mummy ji recited a few complicated Punjabi verses and we stepped out of the house. I smiled and looked at that house from outside, for the first time in my life.

It was still before Sun ji's rise when we reached a place where there was a big crowd with covered heads and folded hands. Though there was a long queue but on seeing me, all the people gave us the way. When we reached at the front, I saw a big book under a small silk canopy and a few people doing very interesting stuff. Two of them were blowing a hand-fan on the big book as if it was a human being, three were playing different musical instruments and the one who I later got to know as *Pathi ji* was reciting verses from the big book. God ji, later on I got to know that it was 'your' home and had a very complicated name called Gurudwara. Unlike our home, your home had no furniture, no kitchen, no radio but just one big room and a lot of guests. Mummy ji took a one rupee note from papa ji and after circulating for seven times above my face, put that in your piggy bank.

From the corner of his left eye, *pathi ji* disapprovingly looked at the one-rupee note and did not even care to give us a second glance. Mama ji, then took out a fifty rupee note and instead of putting it in your piggy bank, kept it on the platform in front of *pathi ji*. There was a big smile on his face and he indicated us to sit on one of the corners of that big room. I was disturbed because I was not enjoying all the attention as in those early days, I was a very reserved person. The other irritating factor was *pathi ji's* loud recitation. He kept on singing the same lines for many minutes and finally invited us when everyone else was gone. He asked mama ji, the purpose of our visit. Mama ji told *pathi ji* that the purpose was to figure out a name for me. *Pathi ji* looked at me and kept his index finger on a random verse in the big book, *"Farz jo tera."*

"The name has to start with 'F'," declared *Pathi ji* and in the same breadth advised, "How about Fateh Singh? The youngest son of Guru Gobind Singh ji, who was buried alive in the wall at Sirhind."

"Very noble, holy and meaningful name," opined mummy ji and looked at papa ji.

Papa ji was looking at a five rupee note which someone half-s heartedly had put in the piggy bank in such a way that it was half in and half out.

"Oh no! He might name me Five Rupees," and the thought of being named like that put so much pressure on me that the yellow semi solid shit again started slipping out of my asshole.

As soon as mummy ji felt that, she alarmed everyone and all of them decided to rush out. Papa ji informed *pathi ji* that they would finalize my name later at home and subsequently let him know.

"But it has to start with 'F'," *Pathi ji* happily announced as mama ji gave him another twenty rupees note while leaving.

As soon as we reached home, mummy ji removed my shorts and put my ass under the hand pump. I stared disrespectfully at her but she did not stop. Thankfully, the water was warm.

After our return from Gurudwara, the entire day was a big torture as everyone around me was behaving unusual. Neither the women were cribbing about neighbors nor the men were gossiping about politics but all were discussing only one thing – 'my to-be name.'

Everyone except mama ji had expressed their opinion by the evening. All hopes were pinned on mama ji because he had done everything right in his life. He had learnt English, settled abroad, earned money and married a fair woman. Moreover, he was the one who had suggested Cute's name which was liked by everyone in Dangar Khera.

All of them were busy in their own world without considering what was going on in my mind. I realized that it was better for me to sleep and dream about my real friends: cows, pigs and cats rather than waste my time listening to them and I fell asleep. I woke up in the evening and before I could even open my sultry eyes, I heard the loud voice of mama ji, '*Behan de* Ramu, where have you died? Get ten glasses immediately."

"Get the drum from the bathroom and mix all these *desi* bottles in that," mama ji ordered our servant Ramu as soon as he reached with those glasses.

Everyone was happy because it was the day when they were going to have *desi* whisky after which mama ji would talk dirty about white aunties. Those were the discussions which all of them cherished and replayed in their minds hundreds of times before discarding and replacing those with the newer ones in mama ji's subsequent trip.

"Jhona ji, tell us about Preeto. Does she still give you signals by rubbing her shoulders against yours?"

"Who Preeto?"

"The white *chikni* who worked in the *kirana* shop. Whom you loved!"

"It is a departmental store and not a *kirana* shop. By the way, her name is not Preeto but Pret and *oye,* she loved me and not I."

"Prait? *Hai hai*, it means Ghosts."

"Hai!"

"Leave all that! For us, she is Preeto. But why does she love you, you are not white?"

"You idiots will never understand, those white *mems* have no other option. Where would they find a Bond like me?"

"Bond? *Hahahhahaha*! Why are you saying that you are a bondd, the *gaand*?"

"*Oye*, useless *kabutar*! Not Punjabi wala bondd but it's the name of the best *angreji* film hero. He is Dara Singh of England. He can do anything. He flies cars, he kills crores of people and he changes his girlfriend every day."

"Yum, yum Jhona ji, you are making our Punjab proud."

"Oye, speak slowly."

"Why speak slowly? I am not afraid of Shammi."

No one in that group except papa ji and mama ji knew that Shammi mami was not at our home but had gone to her parental village.

"What a daring man, Jhona ji! You are great!"

"Jhona ji, you are super *ghaint.*"

"*Ghaint* is fine but does she still rub her shoulders or something more than that?" Kahnu, the *patwari* was madly drunk and was fluttering with desperation to know only about Pret and her shoulders.

"Oye, what do you think of Jhona, I am a man and that too, the most handsome man in Canada. She does everything with your *mitr.*"

Mama ji was loud, boastful, drunk and his words were crystal clear without any hesitation or fumble.

"Everything ???"

"Oye yes, everything."

"Where? In hotel?"

"Why there? Your *mitr* has a five thousand dollar Honda Civic for all these things."

"Really!"

"Waheguru, why did you reproduce us in India? Leave aside white girls, even our wives don't do everything with us now."

"Let's stop this discussion, Jhona ji. Tell me, what to do with *kake's* name?"

Finally, papa ji intervened out of frustration because he was tired of being a bystander. It was only he, who could not participate in that appealing and erotic discussion because no one except him had his wife downstairs to listen to what all they were talking about.

"Jhona ji, you are God! You know so much, why don't you suggest some foreign name for *kake?*"

"A name that *goras* stand up on hearing when he goes to foreign land after he grows old."

"Yes, Jhona ji, something which would make our village proud!"

"So that we can proudly say that we have a boy with an *angreji* name in our village."

"Let me think. How about Fundoo?"

"No Jhona ji, it sounds like *Fuddu*," papa ji replied.

"Fire?"

"It sounds like tyre." Kanhu replied in dissatisfaction.

"Then you find out yourself." Mama ji was upset that both his wonderful names had been turned down by the group.

"Jhona ji, please suggest something which is small and simple."

"Which those *goras* want every day?"

"And which has Punjabi touch."

"Fuck."

"Fuck?"

"Yes, Fuck. It's small and simple, needed by *goras* many a time in a day and has a Punjabi touch as it sounds like truck."

"What a fantastic name, Fuck!"

"Jhona ji, tell us about Preeto now."

"Wait Jhona ji, I am returning in a while."

Papa ji came downstairs, picked up the box of stale *ladoos* bought on the day of my birth and went to our room. Very happily, he put half a *ladoo* in my mouth. I resisted but he pushed that *ladoo* down my throat and then cunningly asked me in English, "What name you, *kake*?"

"Don't you have any shame, *harami*? Why are you coming near your son after getting drunk? Run away or I will break your legs."

"Harmeet, you have the remaining *ladoo*. There is good news; *kake's* name has been finalised."

"What? Fateh?"

"No *Fateh-Shateh* but an English name."

Looking straight in my eyes, he pinched my left cheek with his uncut nailed finger and said, "You is Fuck."

Despite his hurting nails and bad breath, I smiled. I was happy as Fuck sounded much classier than Fateh, Fauji, Fanjeet, Fatti or Favvara, the options which had been discussed since morning.

"Eeh ki naam hoya?"

"Harmeet, *pendu* you, *kake* go foreign in *jawani*, so name English." Papa ji's obsession with English was insatiable.

"Hai, what kind of a name is this Feeeeyyyck? What's the meaning?"

"It's the name of the God of Canada." Without thinking or giving any second thought, he told mummy ji a meaning that she wanted to hear. What an effortless and smooth liar he was!

"Waheguru, waheguru. Fooocck God ji, I am sorry to say ill of you. I did not know that you are the

God of Canada." Mummy ji closed her eyes and recited some verses for a few minutes and asked for forgiveness.

Cybercafé - Day IV

Abnormal School Life

Back in school, life was normal for all but me. Mandal Commission vacations were over and everything that had to settle had settled, but despite trying hard I was not able to get away from my name. Whenever I tried to forget it, someone or the other would remind me of my name. While earlier people used to call me Fuckaiey, Fuckoou, Fuckiiiey or Fuckaaea, now everyone called me Fuck! Just plain Fuck without any prefix or suffix.

In a matter of time, not only my school but the entire village also became deeply obsessed with my name. After initial few weeks, I stopped carrying out fights for my name as that advertised my name even further. Whenever I fought, I used to find my name written on some wall, some blackboard or engraved on one of the benches of the class the next day itself.

God ji, not only the students but my desi teachers also got enlightened about the meaning of my name from other students and started using it for their blissful pleasure.

My trauma used to start with the first activity in the morning – the attendance and would continue until the school's closing bell. From being an interesting activity of announcing the roll numbers and names of students, the attendance became much more painful and torturous involving a lot of remarks about my name. No sooner that our class teacher would announce my name, other students used to shout in Punjabi:

"No fuck in the class Sir ji, only studies."

"Sir ji, fuck is absent, he is only present at night."

"Sir ji, we are too young to have fuck among us."

"Sir ji, fuck is here but surprisingly with clothes."

"Sir ji, today's fuck is different from yesterday's."

"Sir ji, please take fuck out of the class or we will reach Kashmir without going there."

With time, all my classmates were attaining puberty and with puberty, their comments were becoming more and more non vegetarian.

God ji, in no time a full year passed by but still my name did not fade away from students' minds. Initially I was happy at the completion of a year because that meant a good number of twenty-five students of tenth standard who knew my name were passing out of the school but that happiness died the instant I realized that my so called best friends had explained my name to forty-three new students of the first standard. Not only it meant an additional eighteen students knowing my name but also that the student of the first standard who were years away from even learning 'A of apple' were well versed with my four letter long name in the first week of their educational life itself. Seeing that kind of a progress in the young generation, I realized that it was the time I did something about it.

I spent a few months thinking about my options and very intelligently finalized Headmaster ji to be the right homosapien to take my grievance to.

"May I come in, *baba ji*?"

"No!"

"Head *bau ji*, please," I begged.

"Is my office a *dhaba*?"

"No, *saab ji*."

"Then *sabji mandi*?"

"No, sir ji."

"Petrol pump?"

"No ji."

"Then why do you want to come in? All you *madar ch*** students create problems in class and then your *behan ch*** teachers send you to me. Why can't they kick you themselves? Don't they eat ghee?"

"Sir, I am a very very intelligent student and I have been never been sent by any teacher to your office in the history of my school life."

"Every *behan ch*** says this when he comes to my office. Stand outside with both your hands and one leg up for next twenty minutes."

"But *baba ji*?"

"Will you shut up or I make it thirty minutes?"

Headmaster ji was really a terror. His red eyes, red turban and red face turned me red with fear. On that humid afternoon, I stood on just one leg for the next twenty minutes sweating like a pig.

"Ok, your time is up. You may go now."

"But sir ji, I came here to complain about something."

"*Behan ch***, am I an S.H.O. of a police station? Be it teachers, students or even sweepers, everyone comes here to complain. Go and complain to your class teacher."

"But *baba ji*, it's serious. I know your office is not a *dhaba*, a *sabji mandi* or a petrol pump but may I please come in?"

"Oh, you never told me it's serious. I am always there for serious things. Come in."

"Thank you, sir ji. I am in your room today because I want to tell you something. Sir ji, I don't feel like coming to school these days."

"What's serious about this? No one including me wants to come to the school. However, if you seriously don't want to come to school, I can terminate you and you can permanently leave the school."

He had given me the perfect solution. Not only would it save me from the Fuck anthem and other related issues but I could also enjoy unlimited holidays. I was on the verge of saying yes when Headmaster ji said,

"But if you want it, you need to bring papa ji."

"Whose papa ji?"

"*Behan ch***, your papa ji! Who else?

"Sir ji, will any other papa ji do?"

"*Behan ch***, get lost and don't show me your face again till I die."

"Sir ji, please don't do that. I have a serious problem that I want to tell you."

"If it is serious, don't get lost. Tell me about your problem. But believe me, if it's not serious this time, I will make you stand out in the sun for the rest of your life."

"Sir ji, my name is Fuck."

"Such a *kaim* name, I wish I had this name."

"*Baba ji*, don't say this because you don't know the meaning of my name."

"*Kake*, I am the headmaster of the school where you study. I know everything. It means white God of Canada."

"How do you know this?"

"*Kake*, Harmeet told me this when I went to see you on your birth. Didn't she tell you that I even donated five rupees to you?"

"Thank you very much for those five rupees, sir ji but my name does not mean white God of Canada. It means *noonoo-poonoo*."

"Oh *teri*! *Noonoo-poonoo*?"

"Yes sir, *noonoo-poonoo* and the problem is that everyone in the school including all the teachers know this and tease me. I have tried everything from offering lollypop to fights but nothing has restrained them."

"Look *kake*, first of all, a problem as big as this can't be solved by lollypops and second, even if I want, I can't punish the entire school on the basis of your complaint because I don't have enough space outside my room for the entire school to stand on one leg. The problem is you first follow *goras* and keep their names. Later, you complain. Why couldn't you have Fateh Singh or some other name starting with F."

"Sorry sir ji, please forgive my papa ji who always followed goras and agreed to this name. Please give me some solution."

"There is one solution."

"Tell me *baba ji*, tell me!" I asked with impatience, excitement, happiness and courage in my voice.

"Take a knife and cut your ears." after a long pause which seemed very brief, he started laughing, "*Ha ha ha* Fuck, *ha ha ha* Fuck. Now get lost or I will fuck you. *Ha ha ha*."

I did not want to be in his room any longer. Knowing the way he was, he would have even taken a knife and cut my ears had I stayed there even for a minute more.

After my encounter with Headmaster ji, I again went into the mind storming mode for a few days to find a solution to my nomenclature problem but it was in vain.

God ji, it took me another six years to reach the senior most class in the school. There was not a single moment in those six years when I did not curse my mama ji for my name. My name spread like a cow-dung cake fire in the entire village and before I could realize, all the students including the girls, teachers and all their family members knew my name and its meaning.

I never told mummy ji or papa ji about what hot fire I was going through because I was never open with them. Moreover, I was sure that even if I told them, they would have also made fun of me. Had it not been for the letter 'F' that day in Gurudwara, my name and my life would have been something else.

God ji, my journey to the tenth standard was not a pastry-walk. Other than going through the immeasurable harassment associated with my name, I sacrificed a lot to reach there. I had lost many of my friends who had either failed or left studies to pursue other better careers like milking buffaloes, farming or marrying. While Jagga failed in the English exam in ninth standard because he did not know the difference between 'her' and 'here', Ginni left school and went to Jalandhar to learn football to help him secure England's visa and Sukhwinder, in his urge to earn fast money left studies to marry a girl and got a tractor full of dowry. I also lost Ganpat because he failed just once and passed the school by the time I reached matric. Out of our class of thirty-four students in sixth standard, only nineteen students could finally reach the tenth standard.

God ji, among the various professional responsibilities like counting the eggs for mid-day meals, cleaning the playground and planting the trees in the school, the worst assignment of the tenth standard was to address the assembly. Every Monday and Thursday, we used to have assembly in the school when one student of the tenth standard used to read a prayer and which the entire school used to repeat line by line. There were three prayers in our school and all were in English. No one knew the exact reason as to why we had English prayers in a Punjabi school but the fear of speaking English prayer was so high that most of the ninth standard students wished to fail rather than get promoted to the next class.

The turn for the prayer used to come as per the sequence of the roll numbers. The roll numbers in our class were in alphabetical order because of which my roll number was seven and in that one year, I had the stupid luck of leading the prayer not once or twice but four times - 19th August, 17th October, 3rd January and 5th March. My classmates Viraat and Yuvraj because of their roll numbers at the end went through the torture just thrice.

I had dreaded this day for months but 19th August, 1996 finally arrived and that too before my death. I rushed for the local newspaper, Punjab Kesari, first thing in the morning to check if a holiday had been declared because of the death of any Chief Minister, Prime Minister or President the previous night. I checked the front page, middle pages and even sports page but not even a single important person in a population of hundred crores had cared to die on 18th August, 1996.

I got ready and left for school well in advance so that I could help Bhola, our school peon in closing the school quickly in case there was a news of anyone's death. I was the first one to reach the school and had just entered the main gate that I felt myself going into coma. All of a sudden, I could neither move nor talk and I froze. I stood straight like a candle for a few minutes and then fell on the ground. Bhola, who was keeping his toilet cleaning equipment in the storeroom, saw me in that condition and ran to my rescue. He tried to wake me up by first slapping me and then sprinkling contaminated water flowing through the school tap bit I still did not gain consciousness. Since this was not the first time that Bhola was encountering a situation like this and a coma like condition was a common problem with students during the exams, he knew what to do. He used his experienced brain and put his wet rubber slippers fresh out of the school toilet on my nose. It was a familiar smell and my mind reacted positively. I was out of coma instantly. As I opened my eyes, I saw Bhola opening the buttons of my shirt. He was not only a talented sweeper but also had many other virtues.

Despite his busy schedule, he did not leave me midway but kept working on curing the root cause of my problem. He was very focused and completely absorbed in treating me without being bogged down by so many thoughts going on in my mind about him. He rubbed his spit on his palms and then massaged the same on my navel. It was very ticklish and I liked that to the core. I wanted to lie like that and enjoy his massage for years but then I heard a few students getting into the school and had no choice but to get up to avoid being the topic of their dirty jokes. My shirt and shorts got dirty from behind but it did not matter because I was supposed to stand facing others and God ji, as you know when we face others, it's only our front which becomes visible. I saw a flood of students entering the school. All the students got into queues of four and our PT Sir announced my name on the mike, "Prayer by Fukkkk Singh, Roll No 7, Class X A."

I went to the mike and collected the small book of prayers from PT Sir and he whispered, "Prayer number two."

I took the prayer book in my hand and said, "Good …"

Everyone was staring at me which made me go weak in my knees. I closed my eyes and started again,

"Good Morning, *sangat ji*."

The start was slightly wrong as I had to refer the audience as students and not *sangat ji* because it was a school and not a Gurudwara. Nobody cared and like a pre-recorded audio tape, they replied, "Good morning, Fuck *veer ji*."

"I, Fuck here, today to distribute prayer. First, I speak and then same to same, you speak."

"We don't want prayer, we want fuck," someone shouted in Punjabi from the back row.

"Fuck is our god, fuck is our religion and fuck is our prayer," this time it was someone from the middle row.

The mention of my name by those sacrilegious students made me so uneasy that I forgot whatever I had rehearsed. I kept quiet for some time, assembled my thoughts in Punjabi, translated those Punjabi words to English and continued, "today's prayer page 7 from is…"

"Today's prayer Page 7 from is…," entire school diligently followed me.

This was my mistake; how could I forget that they were a bunch of unintelligent, illiterate, repetitive students? Those brainless creatures even lacked the capability to realize that they had to repeat only the prayer and not the introduction. However, it was my foolishness that I over expected from them. They did not deserve that nice and intelligent introduction. I directly started the prayer,

"God's love."

"God's love."

Though I had chorused that prayer at least a few crore times in my school life but speaking the same in front of others was a very enlightening and spiritual experience.

I continued the prayer,

"'is so wonderful."

"'is so wonderful."

"fill in the blank 3."

"fill in the blank 3."

"It is not 'fill in the blank 3' but it means you need to speak this line three times like the way I am going to speak your name now, *Khota, Khota ,Khota*." PT Sir shouted from where he was standing.

The entire school started laughing and my brain boiled. PT Sir was not a teacher but a washer man. How could he call me *Khota* in front of the entire school and that too thrice when it was not my fault? God ji, how would one read something written as 'God's love is so wonderful _ 3'. My boiling mind advised me to tear the prayer book and throw the pages on PT Sir's face but I took a deep breath and finished the prayer in one go.

"Oh! Wonderful love! So high, you can't get over it; so high, you can't get over it; so high, you can't get over it,

Oh! Wonderful love!, So deep, you can't get under it; so deep, you can't get under it; so deep, you can't get under it,

Oh! Wonderful love!, So wide, you can't get around it; so wide, you can't get around it, so wide, you can't get around it. Oh! Wonderful love!"

A few students tried to repeat what I spoke but since most of them were shorter than me, they did not have breaths as big as mine to match my pace. No sooner than I finished the prayer, I got a very heavy slap from PT Sir. Many students used to think that PT Sir's slap weighed four kilograms and I never believed them but after eating that slap, I was sure that if not four kilograms then it was at least five kilograms.

"Son of a donkey, bend down and become a *murga.*"

"Sir ji, please don't do this. I am in tenth standard and I am mature."

"Fukkkk, become a *murga* in one second or you will have your lunch in Civil Hospital today."

I knew that the Civil Hospital's food was terrible and I would have preferred death over that so putting my tenth standard ego aside, I immediately bent down and became a *murga.*

God ji, one thing had become very clear when I was in tenth standard; very few students in my class had the aura. While my papa ji and mummy ji could never recognize my true potential, there was one person who was able to see the invisible circle of knowledge around me, our English teacher R.K. Sharma Sir. He was not only our English teacher but our class teacher in charge and had a special place for a genius like me in his heart. He was a new teacher in our school and had been transferred from Government Middle School, Fazilka. He had been transferred out of his hometown because he had missed attending the *sangat darshans* of the Education Minister ji to get his transfer cancelled.

God ji, I am sure that you would be interested in knowing more about the *sangat darshans* because this is a practice inspired from your habit of giving *darshan* to your followers. It was a practice started by the ministers of Punjab a few years ago. They would give their *darshan* to the normal humans of Punjab time to time. Not only could one get one's problems resolved from the supreme authority of the land but one would also be served *langar* at the end of the *sangat darshan*.

It had just been a month that R. K. Sharma Sir had become our teacher in charge that an unprecedented thing happened. One of my classmates, Mota passed away to Naya Nangal. His father worked for Public Works Department. Since he had worked in Abohar office for more than a decade, the government decided to move him away and with this, moved our class monitor of nine years. There was a power vacuum and an utter chaos in our class. There was no one to write the names of the talkative students on the blackboard, to clean the litter of the classroom, to collect the homework notebooks or to complain the teachers about the actual condition of the students on sick leave. In the absence of a monitor, we all turned wild and proclaimed 'forceful self-rule' by forcing ourselves on the other students of the class. We all knew that this could not continue and eventually a monitor would be appointed so every morning before the first period, someone or the other used to go to Sharma Sir to collect chalks and duster so as to impress him for the coveted monitorship.

Finally, good sense prevailed over him and on an action packed Friday morning, he took everyone by surprise when he announced his decision to appoint a new monitor. By luck, I was sitting on the first bench because I had reached late in the class and all the back-benches were occupied before I reached. To my un-timeliness, Neetu was also late and she sat beside me. Before I could even notice Neetu's clothes or smell her hair, Sharma ji arrived for the first period and in his usual missile style fast-paced tone said, "*Bachho*, who wants to be the monitor of this class?"

Everyone except Neetu and Keeri raised their hands. Though all of us had our lips tightly sealed but inside our brain we were loudly praying to get that coveted position. While we were waiting with raised hands for Sharma Sir to choose one of us, he was squeezing both his eyes with his thumb and forefingers.

"Oh! Where did I forget my spectacles?"

It was not the first time that he had forgotten something. Though he was a 'bomb' English teacher, he had a bad memory. Except English language, he had practically forgotten everything at one point or the other in last one month that he was at our school. He had forgotten his pen, his watch, his attendance register and now his spectacles also. Kulbir being a smart, opportunist and a buttery guy went to him and offered his spectacles but Sharma ji's tomato shaped face was much wider than Kulbir's carrot shaped face. As soon as he tried wearing that pair of spectacles, it broke into three pieces. If this was not enough, now Kulbir became Sharma Sir's counterpart in being blind as well.

"Oh, so we have only one student who is interested in becoming the monitor," he said squeezing his eyes, standing half a feet away from me.

"What's your name?"

Nobody knew who he was talking to, but his head, eyes, nose were all pointing toward me.

"Fockk *kaka*!" Neetu was more excited than me in announcing my name.

"I Sir, I Sir," shouted many students but Sharma ji saw only my aura and heard only Neetu's words.

"Fockk! What is this name?"

"Sir ji, it means the process to make a child." Neetu was trying her best not to let anyone else speak and spoil my chance.

I wanted to tell him that I was Fuck and not Fockkk but in the absence of his spectacles, he would have not understood. I kept quiet.

"This is a class and not a maternity hospital. I can't make someone with such a difficult name, the monitor. Moreover, it's a very sentimental name as my wife and me have not been to make a baby in the last thirteen years of our marriage." He started crying from the top of his naked, un-spectacled eyes.

Though Sharma Sir's cried very loudly, the number of tears were way below expectation. Despite trying hard, he was able to emit only four tears but those tears were good enough for Neetu to use her charm and impress him. She took out her white *dupatta* and started wiping his tears. While she was looking at Sharma Sir and mopping his eyes, the entire class including Sharma Sir was watching her two big milk-plants which in the absence of *dupatta* were looking even bigger and round. For a while, no one was praying to become the monitor but only wishing for Sharma Sir's eyes to continue tearing for ages to come. While we were all eyes, Neetu was all words. She moved further closer to Sharma Sir and said,

"If you do proper Fockk, you don't need thirteen years but even thirteen months are good enough. Please make him the monitor and his name will keep on reminding you on what to do and I promise that you will make a child in no time."

God ji, if you were in Sharma Sir's shoes, even you would have agreed to whatever Neetu would have asked you.

"Ok, so Fockkk is your new monitor."

Finally, for the first time in my life someone got me something because of my name and not despite my name. I was so happy that I pinched Neetu on her big, fat buttocks to express my happiness. I would not have dared to pinch her earlier on her buttocks but that moment onwards, I could do that because I was the class monitor of Class X-A and any girl in the world would have felt blessed to be pinched on her buttocks by me.

God ji, if you think that becoming the monitor was the happiest phase of my school life and everything fell in place after that, then like the time you mistrusted your wife Sita ji by asking her to go through fire, you are wrong this time too. I had become the monitor of the class but except Neetu, I had lost my control on rest of the students.

All the male students in order to take revenge from me for surpassing them in becoming the monitor made a group with an English name called 'Fuck the Fuck'. The responsibility of each of the group members was to execute one horrible activity every week using my name to make me pee in my pants. I could never find out who made that group but it must have been some pig from the previous life because the group's accomplishments were excessively dirty. For starters, they modified all the prevalent abuses with my name. *'Teri behan nu fuck'* and *'Teri maa nu fuck'* became common phrases replacing the age-old traditional proverbs in our school. Once these expressions got committed to everyone's memory, they changed the name of the sharpener to 'Fuck' and 'I need a fuck to sharpen my pencil' became a popular idiom. They even coined 'May I fuck in?' instead of 'May I come in?' for seeking permission from teachers like Bulla Singh Sir who were equally *harami* like students. 'Fuck the Fuck' members not only restricted their actions to our school but they also did their best to spread my name in the entire village.

Not only punjabi graffitis with my English name like 'Keep your sisters away from the Fuck or you will become mama', 'Use mustard oil when you face Fuck or you will cry in pain' and 'Fuck is our class monitor but he is still missing from our lives' decorated many of the village walls but a few places like the platform around *anaj mandi* also was used for painting a big Shiv Lingam of yours with my name written on it. God ji, while all these little things were nothing in comparison of the joy of being a monitor, what hurt me the most was the use of my name in the village *Ram Leela*.

God ji, while you started *Ram Leela* to showcase your history to the world, over time these have become the narratives of unholy, triple meaning fun-filled tales and that year, it touched new unscalable peaks when my class students used my name for one of the characters. They named one repulsive looking monkey in Hanuman ji's military as Fuck and for the entire two hours of *Ram Leela,* he would do nothing but wear black goggles and tell everyone from Ram ji to Lakshman ji in a loud breathless tone, "Don't fuck Raavan ji but fuck me because I am Fuck," to which everyone would reply, "We don't fuck monkeys."

God ji, with all this backstabbing I went into seclusion and left friendship with everyone except Neetu but as the days passed, I got fed up as I could not tolerate talking only to Neetu all the time. The problem with her was not only her frequent use of the word '*kake*' but her brain. God ji, I think you constructed her brain wearing a microscope on your eyes because in normal situation you would not have been able to make such a small brain.

God ji, Neetu's brain because of its small size could think of only three things - her clothes, her mummy ji's food and her hatred-laden words for Keeri. While I found the discussions about her beautiful salwar suits and tiffin to be intelligent, I did not like her talking bad about Keeri. God ji, the reason that she spoke bad about Keeri was not historical but a very recent development which had happened in their lives. Neetu and Keeri were best friends till 4th July, 1996 but things changed drastically on that day and they became the worst of enemies after that. It all started on 1st July, 1996 when Neetu's papa ji went to Pathankot to attend a wedding of a young daughter of his old friend. The wedding was on 2nd July so Neetu's papa ji boarded the overnight bus a day before to reach early on the day of the wedding. He was so excited for the wedding that he wore a brown shirt and black trouser stitched by Wear Well Tailors, Abohar.

Everything was just fine for him till the morning of 2nd July when all of a sudden, he started sneezing. The culprit was the chilled Coca Cola served to him as a welcome drink which he didn't have a habit of drinking. Unable to recover, he consulted his friend who being a poultry farm owner suggested him to have a few boiled eggs from his farm free of cost to eliminate the ill effect of Coca Cola. Neetu's papa ji ate fourteen eggs in two hours but still nothing improved. In a state of shock and without attending the wedding, he took the afternoon bus from Pathankot and reached Dangar Khera late at night on 3rd July. Upon his arrival, he was immediately offered the hot milk of his own buffalo which he happily drank and then slept for four hours. To everyone's happiness, he had forgotten sneezing when he woke up on 3rd July. With a relaxed state of mind; he took bath, ate seven *paranthas* and slept again. Neetu woke him up in the evening and asked for Kashmiri apples. Her papa ji asked for forgiveness as he could not manage to get those apples from Pathankot because of his ill health.

Neetu cried all evening but finally, with the joint efforts of her mummy ji, papa ji, elder *veer ji* and *bhabhi ji*, she understood, stopped crying and ate *matar-paneer* for dinner before sleeping. Next day, she explained everything to Keeri who had also requested for those apples. Keeri refused to accept her argument as she was sure that Neetu was lying and had ate her share of apples too. They had an intense argument and after the third period, when both of them were returning from *Janana* toilet, Keeri slapped Neetu. Subsequent to that slap, both of them broke their best friendship, even without saying the customary *katti*. When I asked Neetu if Keeri had washed her hands before slapping her, she laughed at me and said, "Fockkk *kake*, you don't even know this! Girls do not need to wash their hands after they urinate." Though I did not understand the rationale but I still believed her.

Two months after I became the monitor, I became desperate to get my normal life back but without leaving the plum post that I was holding. I was not able to find out a way to balance my desire of controlling the class and still being friendly with them. I thought of asking my elders for a solution but that would have made me look like a brinjal who has the crown but no leadership capabilities. That might also have become a roadblock in my becoming the 'Father of Punjab' in future. Other than the option of consulting elders, I just had two more ways to figure out the solution of my dilemma. First, to introspect and find the solution from the age-old wisdom of seventeen years of my life and second, to refer to ever-knowledgeable Punjab Kesari.

Since I did not want to put too much stress on my already strained mind, I opted for the second option and for next three days after my school, I went to Devi Dyal's *kabadi* shop and read all the bigger font headlines of around thirteen Punjab Kesari(s). I knew Devi Dyal very well because he was our family *kabadi* and our family had been selling old newspapers at Rs.4 per kilogram, empty whisky bottles at Re.1 per bottle and rusted iron scrap at Rs.12 per kilogram to him since my birth. Papa ji used to sell bottles and scrap to Devi Dyal's father before my birth. He did not have newspapers because my family subscribed to newspaper only after I was born. Maybe the birth of a well-educated child who was to become the monitor of Class X-A of Government High School, Dangar Khera was big enough a pressure for a stingy man like my papa ji to start spending Rs.1.25 every day on the newspaper. I am sure Devi Dyal used to mint a lot of money because the price of new Punjab Kesari went up from Rs.1.25 to Rs.2.50 by the time I reached the tenth standard but the price of old newspaper remained fixed at Rs.4 only. Had I fathered an intelligent son like me, I would have definitely seduced him to become a *kabadi* but unfortunately, my papa ji did not have that wisdom.

There were three news items in those old Punjab Kesari(s) which helped me find the best solution for my problem. While two of the news, about the Home Minister and the Agriculture Minister were from the black and white boring pages, the third and the most insightful news was from Thursday's colored filmi pullout.

Kala Kachha Gang Back In Action

Ladhuka (Dhingra): May 13

After a gap of almost two months, the Kala Kachha gang of thieves is back in action, this time with a lot more energy, bigger group size and a never before vengeance. Last night, eleven of them attacked the house of Kulwant Singh Beeba, a famous rice seller of Ladhuka village of Fazilka sub division and looted three cows, five *tolas* gold jewellery and three Atlas cycles. Luckily, everyone was sleeping so there was no violence as knowing Kulwant Singh, had he been awake, he would have surely used his gun. Sardar Tota Singh, the Home Secretary of Punjab, who is currently in America to attend the Punjabi Conclave has asked DSP of Fazilka, Mr. Hoshiar Singh to put at least three hundred thieves behind the bars in next thirty days. The idea is to break their unity. Their unity is their strength and breaking it is critical.

Cotton Prices Soar Higher

Mandi Kotakpura (Pritam): Sep 14

Dhansukh Bansal of Faridkot is very happy these days. The wealthiest commission agent of the region says that he has never seen the prices of cotton this high. As per his estimate, the cotton prices will go further up by another 300 rupees per bail. However, not everyone in this cotton belt is happy. Cotton farmers from the region held a big dharna outside Agriculture

Minister, Choudhary Naib Singh's residence in Batala demanding his intervention in getting them a better cotton price from the commission agents who have made a cartel and are pocketing major profits themselves. Naib Singh, who was in Batala to attend the wedding of his nephew, has warned commission agents of dire consequences if they don't mend their ways and has asked the Agriculture Minister to investigate the matter.

Raveena Tandon Says No to Bikini

Mumbai (Agencies)

The glamour doll of Bollywood has denied media reports about wearing bikini in her next movie. The *mast mast* girl says that she would never do movies which people can't watch with their families. On being asked about her romance with Akshay Kumar and the rumours of their marriage, she reiterated that they were just a good onscreen pair and nothing more. She said 'no comments' when asked about the increasing number of kissing scenes in her movies.

God ji, the essence of these news items widely opened my eyes and taught me three important lessons to rule the class. From the first two news, I got a perspective on how big leaders work. I learnt that unlike other professionals such as teachers, postmen or clerks, big leaders themselves don't work on all the things. They spend their energy on happy things like traveling abroad and attending marriages rather than wasting their time on problems. Their only job in the times of crisis is to order their subordinates to handle the situations.

While the first two news items were good, it was the third news which was most helpful in laying the foundation stone of a future leader in me. God ji, you are a bit aged so you might not understand but Raveena Tandon ji was a '*maal*' in those days. It does not mean that she is not a '*maal*' now but of late, she hardly sends her photographs to Punjab Kesari and even on those rare occasions when she does, her photographs are in un-filtered clothes. On the top of it, newspapers also have turned sober and don't write erotic adjectives like *mast-mast* or *tip-tip* girl for her which makes her news avoidable to read. However, it does not mean that there is a drought in newspapers as these days we have some other options. These days most of the Punjabi villagers get to read about another young, hot, seductive, smart, intelligent, faithful, homely girl - Rakhi Sawant ji.

God ji, while Raveena Tandon ji's news was smaller than the first two but don't go by the size as it was the most educational of them all. In a few lines, it imparted in me quintals of wisdom and changed me from being 'just another monitor' to the icon of the school. I got two important morals from Raveena Tandon ji's story. First, to let my classmates know that Neetu and I were just in-class students and nothing more. This would help me in becoming friends with Keeri's admirers who had started hating me. My second learning was to be polite to everyone and say 'no comments' whenever I faced a complicated situation.

God ji, it was on a Saturday evening that I got enlightenment and therefore, I could not sleep peacefully for two nights as I was doing dress rehearsal in my dreams for what I was going to do in the class on Monday. I decided to utilize the Drawing period on Monday to deliver my controlling lecture as I had lost interest in drawing years ago- the day Jhujhar told me that it were the brokers and not the painters who earned more money from selling art.

On that Monday morning, as was the custom, five minutes into the Drawing period and our drawing teacher Chawla Sir asked us to copy a yellow snake from the black board and left for the staff room, leaving the class in my custody. Yellow snake along with the red ant was his favorite which he had made years ago on the black board and had been asking students to copy that in all his classes since then- red ant for the junior students and yellow snake for the senior ones. Chawla Sir had a very extrovert style of teaching as he never spent more than five minutes in any of his classes.

Once he left the class to me, I waited for everyone to finish their yellow snake. All the students because of their experience of five years made that snake in just thirty minutes by drawing two parallel lines and coloring it with the yellow color. While they were scheming on what to do in the remaining ten minutes of the period, I was re-rehearsing in my mind the most powerful speech ever delivered by any class monitor.

"Neetu, come with me to the black board," I whispered in her earlobes while she was absorbed in giving finishing touch to her snake.

"Let me first make the eyes of the snake."

"Leave it. Anyway, Chawla Sir will ask me to check these sheets. Don't worry."

"My Fockkk *kake,* you look so mast when you talk all this. This monitor-y is your real *tashan*," saying that she came with me to the black board. I took out a thread from my short's pocket and loudly asked Neetu to tie that on my right wrist.

"This is a kite thread, *kake*. Why do you want me to tie it on your hand? Do you want me to fly you like a kite?"

"No, Neet Kaur. He wants you to tame him like your buffalo."

"Ha ha ha," "Ha ha ha," "Ha ha ha."

"Shut up, Ghuggi," ordering that I went straight to him and tore his drawing sheet. His ferocious yellow snake got cut into pieces even before its color could dry.

"Shut up class and listen. This thread is rakhi and from today, Neetu is my sister."

"*Teri maa nu* Fockk. Why you? You are not *Maharaja Patiala*, I don't want to be your sister. Select someone else from the class as your sister."

"Why someone else? When it's the time to eat *jalebi* and *samosa*, it's you and when it's the time to make a sister, it's someone else. *Khabardaar,* Fuckkey! If you come closer to me," Keeri could not control her anger at Neetu's remarks.

"*Naa ji, naa*, he never ever got me a single *samosa* or *jalebi*. It's me who pays every time as Fockkk always says that his papa ji never gives him money. If you have any doubt, ask the canteen *paaji*."

"He did the same to me in 6ᵗʰ standard," Cheeku got up and said.

"To me last year as well," Gaba also joined them.

"Gali gali main truck hai, hamara manitar Fuck hai,

Gali gali main shor hai, hamara manitar chor hai."

Bunty raised the slogan and slowly, the entire class including Neetu joined him.

"Fuck karo Fuck nu ajj," someone shouted from the last bench. I panicked. I had to do something or they would beat me up. I immediately took the chalk and started writing the names of the disturbing students on the black board in full speed.

Ghuggi, Cheeku, Gaba, Morr, Nirmal, Keeri…

With each name the noise kept on reducing and by the time I wrote two more names, the entire class turned silent.

"I will give the names of the noisy students to Headmaster ji if you start again."

I went to the last bench where Paramvir sat to check the time. There were only two students in our class who had watch - Paramvir and Nirmal. However, I preferred Paramvir because unlike Nirmal's watch with fingers, his watch had numbers and was easy to comprehend. God ji, it did not mean that one could understand time from Paramvir's watch without applying any brain as it needed ample intelligence to understand whether it was 'A.M.' or 'P.M' which was a very difficult task, especially on cloudy and rainy days.

It was 12.23 by his watch. I looked outside and it was sunny. I immediately knew it was 12.23 P.M and there were only seven minutes left for the period to finish.

"Sardar Honey, Bablu, Gullu, Manu, Cheeku, Ghuggi, Paramvir, Gaba, Viraat, Nirmal, Yuvraaj, Sardarni Neetu and Keeri."

"Why are you taking our *kuchcha* names?" Bablu whose school name was Balwinder, protested against me using nicknames.

"*Kaminey*, will you keep quiet or you want me to tell your *pakka* name to Headmaster ji?"

I started having second thoughts about whether these rural people, who could not even sit quietly, deserved my intelligent speech at all but then I thought of my future as 'Father of Punjab' when I would have to distribute my speeches to crores of rural people like them. So, I continued…

"Other than announcing Neetu as my sister, I have two more announcements to make. First announcement is that from today five of you namely Manu, Yuvraaj, Neetu, Cheeku and Gullu will be my secretaries. Second and the most important announcement is that no one will tell about the appointments of secretaries to Sharma Sir and if anyone dares to tell him, all the remaining secretaries will crush him like a big elephant crushes the small ants."

All the secretaries were extremely happy and started clapping. It was the biggest day of their life. All was going as per my dress rehearsal but then Neetu asked, "Fockkk *kake*, what would be the work of the secretaries?"

It was a very difficult question and I had never thought that someone would ask me this. I smilingly said, "No comments."

"Can I give this news to my family and neighbors?" Manu asked.

"No comments."

"Will we get extra marks in exams for being the secretary?"

"No comments."

Before they could ask more of those complicated questions, Bhola heard the desire of my heart and started hammering the bell to announce the end of the period. I immediately collected the yellow snake sheets and rushed to the staff room.

God ji, my life changed completely after that day and all my classmates became my friends. Secretaries became my friends because they were indebted to me for giving them the opportunity of their life and non-secretaries became my friends because they had a hope that someday, my eyes would fall on them and they would also get a chance to become the secretaries. Only Neetu was a little frigid initially but with time she also changed as she realized that being my sister was just a small price to pay for becoming the secretary of class X-A. My journey as the monitor was very smooth after that. My studies also improved and by the grace of my hard work and brain, I cleared the board exams of the tenth standard in the first attempt with jealous-able 37% marks.

Cybercafé -Day V

Sant Singh College, Abohar

God ji, there are two kinds of people in Dangar Khera – nervous and confident. While nervous ones never become confident, the confident ones sometimes turn nervous and that's exactly what happened to me after I cleared 10th standard. All of a sudden, I realized that there was no further class in my school and the reason for the same was the unstable politics of India. While Indian politics had never affected me till then, it changed my life in a major way when the then Prime Minister of India, Mr. H.D Deve Gowda ji resigned from his Prime Ministership a month before my board results. Though we got his replacement very quickly and Mr. I.K. Gujral became our new Prime Minister but it still disturbed the course of my career. We were very happy the day Gujral ji became our Prime Minister. We felt extremely proud because our Punjabi *veer ji* got that position. Since he was from Punjab, I was sure that one of the first policy announcement from his office would be to stretch our school to 12th standard. To my horror, he did not do that. I really got angry at his inability but in retrospect, I don't think it was entirely his fault but the fault of thousands of *halwais* across the geometry of Punjab. God ji, whenever someone becomes Prime Minister from Punjab, all the Punjabi sweet-makers start making *ladoos* for days and weeks at a stretch. It's not that they make *ladoos* for themselves or for their family members but for the political party workers. God ji, please don't think that I am comparing you with anyone but for political party workers it's not 'you' but Prime Minister ji, who is their God. The way you like *karaah* in Gurudwaras, *boondi* and *peda* in temples and candles in church, Prime Minister ji likes *ladoos* and as soon as they become the Prime Minister, all the party workers take 500 gram to 1kilogram boxes of *ladoos* for them and force feed them.

Being the monitor of my class, I was so busy in my work that I failed to notice all these political developments and got extremely confused about my future the day I got my 10th result. It would have been easier had I failed because then I would have enrolled in the same class in the same school and by your blessings would have even become the same monitor once again. Alas! I had passed and that too with flying marks because of which I was shocked and in terrible need of advice. There was no point in taking papa ji's advice because by then I knew him in and out to understand that he was the most un-advisable person. Mummy ji, on the other hand, was worthy of taking advice but I knew that she would tell me to consult papa ji so I did not ask her also. After remaining worried for three long days, I decided to approach the most intellectually sensitive person of my school and I went to see Bhola.

Bhola lived behind the school because his 'home sweet home' was there. He had one fresh wife as he had got married a year back. Bhola must have selected his wife after thorough analysis because she was very fair and very pulpy, the kind of dream wife everyone wanted but only a few could have. One of the reasons she married Bhola was he was very stylish and that was obvious from the entrance of his small home. It had a big wooden nameplate, better than the one outside Principal Sir's room.

- Mr. Bhola Sahni, Government Jamadaar (Permanent)

- Mrs. Mala Sahni, Wife (New)

His fashionable bicycle with decorated wheel rims was parked outside his hut and to add to style, he had a doorbell too. I wanted his wife to open the door. I had seen her only once when she came to our school after her marriage and I had been dreaming of talking to her since then. As soon as I pressed the bell, I sensed someone running toward the door and as soon as the door opened, I felt someone jumping at me and kissing me. I felt so shy that I closed my eyes and the kissing turned to biting. I fell on the ground but before I could reciprocate, I heard a lady shouting, "run away from him, Billa has gone *halka*."

God ji, your world is very antonym-ic. When men turn mad, they become harmless but when dogs become mad or *halka*, they infest so many worms that only twelve painful injections and those too on the stomach do the justice of de-worming.

By the time I regained my audio- video senses, I realized that Bhola's pet dog Billa had turned mad after eating some poisonous weeds and as was the tradition of the dying *halka* dogs, he was hungry to bite whosoever he could lay his teeth on. I was the first and the second last target in his biting mission as he died soon after biting an old uncle ji who was enjoying his time smoking *hukka* while sitting on his *charpoy* in that lane. Though it was my first and last meeting with Billa but it left un-forgetful marks, especially on my face. Lying there on the ground, I had not even come out of the traumatic taste of biting that I got another filthy blow, this time on my moral fibre when beautiful Mala Sahni ji asked,

"*Veer ji*, are you ok?"

God ji, how would you feel if after a long wait, the two apsaras Miss Meneka Ji and Miss Rambha ji come to meet you and ask, "*Veer ji*, are you ok?" Everything was happening in a wrong way and I knew the reason. The fault was mine as I had kept my slippers facing upside down before sleeping the previous night. Before sleeping, I heard one of our beautiful buffaloes' moan and unwillingly, I ran to take some action as I had been forcibly made in-charge of them as soon as I finished my 10th standard exams. I wore my fateful slippers, took out my Reynolds pen from the steel almirah and rushed toward the buffaloes' lounge. The moaning stopped as soon as I switched on the lounge's bulb with the help of my pen. I waited for five minutes but all the buffaloes acted to be fast asleep and no one made even an ounce of sound.

Though the suspect was the light brown buffalo as she was partially awake and had a wry smile on her foamed mouth but I was still not sure about the culprit. I was angry beyond imagination at those illiterate and junk buffaloes to spoil the sleep of an erstwhile monitor. I wanted to beat all of them but they were six and I was alone and that too in half sleep. I left them unbeaten. Feeling helpless, I returned to my room but in that stupid trip, I forfeited my feet, my *pyjama* and my slippers to the mud. I removed my *pyjama*, threw that in the verandah for mummy ji to wash the next day and cleaned my feet and slippers with the water flowing out of our hand pump. Though I used my bed sheet to dry my feet but I kept the slippers upside down on the floor to let them dry. I had been ordered lacs of times by *dadi ji* not to do that but since I was mentally disturbed because of my insult by the buffaloes, I did not care about the old lady's prophecies. As soon as I woke up the next day, I realized that I had committed a big mistake and was sure that things that day would go the opposite way for me. Had I not been an ex-monitor, I would have thrown those slippers in the sewer and remained bare foot my entire life but I was a celebrity and could not do that as I had my 'status' to maintain. I was down in dust but still I had a hope- the hope of talking to Mala ji. I managed to get up and followed Mala ji into her house.

"*Ha ha ha*, Billa is very naughty. Even in a normal state, he never leaves the guests un-injured and now that he is poisoned, this is the bare minimum damage which he could have caused," shouted Bhola while coming out from one of the rooms of his house, the same room in which Mala ji had just entered.

"Bhola, you were inside! Why did you not save me from that beast?"

"Because Billa is not my dog. My wife got him along with her when we got married. You don't know women; if I had saved you then she would have got angry at me for not letting her dog eat what he wanted."

"But it was she who asked me to run away?"

"That was to protect her dog from you and not the other way round. Her only worry was Billa. In fact, even now she is sitting inside and crying as she is worried about her dog."

It was becoming unbearable for me to tolerate Mala ji's crying anymore as that was making me *halka* so I got up and said, "Bhola, I am leaving now."

"But take your salary at least" and he took out a five rupee note from his pocket and handed that over to me.

"What salary?" Though I was happy and excited with that sum of money in my hand but call it destiny or the curse of inverted slippers that my tongue moved in haste and said those two words.

"Oh! You are not the son of the chowkidar Balbir? He comes on this date every month to collect the salary on his father's behalf."

God ji, you know that I am very smart but either it was because of my broken heart or my broken face that my neck automatically moved from left to right and from right to left and even before I could realize, he snatched that expensive five rupee note from my hands.

"Then who are you and what are you doing here?"

"Bhola, you don't remember me, I am the historic monitor of class 10th A, Fuck Singh."

"Oh yes! But you look so different."

"Yes, it's because of Billa's marks on my face."

"I know; he has the sharpest set of teeth in the world and that too without ever brushing those. *Ha ha ha*" and then he curiously asked, "Is it correct that your name means what everyone else says?"

God ji, this was a tricky question and I faced it a few times every day. I knew that he knew the meaning of my name but was still asking to get some naughty excitement at my cost so I used my age-old, many a time practiced reply.

"How can others know the correct meaning of my name? It's my name and it's me who knows its meaning. It means the white God of Canada."

"Hmmm! Fuck Singh, don't go by my name and think that I am that *bhola*. This white God story will not work with me. Feel at home, don't feel shy and tell me the real meaning of your name."

God ji, there was magic in his words. Despite trying my best, I could not resist his charm and told him the truth. No sooner than I told him the truth, the truth which he already knew, he got angry and said,

"How dare you come to my home with such an erotic name knowing completely well that I am married to the very beautiful Mala Sahni. What would I tell her if she asks me who came? Now please get lost and never come to my place of residence again."

"But I have some very important work with you and I will not leave before finishing that."

"Nothing is more important to me than my married life and your presence here is not at all healthy for that. Please finish whatever you have to say in next one second and run away from here."

"Bhola ji, I am undergoing the biggest problem of my life. I have passed my 10th standard exam and I can no longer go to the school." I even thought of reminding him of all those memories which he and I shared but one second was too little to remind him all about it.

"I am sorry, Fuck Singh, that you can no longer go to our sensuous school. But now that you have passed the tenth standard, what do you plan to do?"

"That's why I am here because you have been the peon of the school for so many years and you have seen a lot of prodigious students like me passing tenth standard. Though I know that they were not as intelligent as me but you can still guide me from their experience of what they did after graduating from the school."

"Fuck, I am not sure why you came here but let me tell you that if you also came to me like many of your old seniors to know the secret of 'how to become a government peon?' then you are mistaken. I will tell that secret to my own personal children only and not to anyone else."

"But is it possible for me to become a government peon like you?" Though I always wanted to be the Father of Punjab but seeing his house, his style and above all his wife, I got so mesmerized that for a moment my dream changed to become a government peon.

"No! Not even if I tell you the secret because it is only the privilege of my family," shouting that he held my left hand and took me to one of those two rooms, the one without his wife and made me stand in front of four passport size photographs pasted on an old piece of mirror.

"He is Mola Ram, the first generation peon of my family. He started his career as a cobbler but one day an old Britisher got so impressed on seeing the shoe polish and the cleaning brush in his hand that he bestowed him with the assignment of his personal peon. Next to him is Tola Ram who even surpassed his father's milestone and became the favorite peon of the

Magistrate of Ferozepur. He was so good as a peon that Magistrate ji often used to prefer him over his wife for many a chore. Other two stalwarts in this frame are Chola Ram and Kola Ram. Chola Ram was born with a silver spoon as the son of Magistrate's peon and became so spoilt that he even recruited another peon for himself. Though he did not become a great peon but his son and my papa ji, Kola Ram broke all records. People say that my papa ji was so good that British even requested Pandit Nehru ji to dispatch him to England but Nehru ji being a true preserver of quality, never let it happen. Fuck Singh, it's not just the secret but you even need to have a lineage to become a government peon. So, don't even dream of becoming one."

"So, what do I do?"

"Go and study at Sant Singh College and then try becoming a graduate. That's a much easier thing to do."

Though I was hurt by his and Malaji's unloving attitude towards me but I still did not decide not to attend their funerals if they died before me because my objective was achieved. If not love, at least I got my career direction in that meeting. Bhola had tipped me to become a graduate. Though he did not tell me but I knew for sure that there was some great underlying hidden opportunity in becoming a graduate which he would disclose once I cleared graduation. Intelligent people like Bhola never advised anything just for the sake of advising because he had the generations of peon-wisdom in his blood. I absorbed his advice, went to Krishna Medical Hall to get myself injected for dog bites and mesmerized everyone in my family in the evening by disclosing to them my decision of becoming a graduate.

Everyone was happy but as usual papa ji had one pre-condition. He would let me pursue Bhola's dream of studying in Sant Singh College only if I took over his responsibility of thirty acres of sugarcane farms in addition to taking care of the buffaloes. I resisted but his stupid logic was that if he could start taking care of them at the age of ten, I should also arrive in life and ease his young shoulders off those two burdens so that he could focus and spend his time more constructively on whisky and other related activities.

The tradeoff was unjustifiable, oppressive and cruel but I agreed as I had read enough about Bhagat Singh Ji in my school - one chapter each in English, Hindi and Punjabi textbooks and that had made me strong enough to handle tyrants like papa ji.

Next day, Ghuggi and I took the bus to Abohar and applied for admission to the first and last college of my life. The admission process was very easy except that there was one major confusion. Unlike my school where I was allocated subjects, I had to choose my own subjects in the college. I asked a few other students for help but there was no consensus among them. Some of them suggested me to go for Medical Science while others were in favor of Commerce and a few even told me the benefits of Non-medical and Humanities. The clerk at the application counter advised me to choose the combination of my favorite subjects. Though I was very good at studies but I never had any favorite subject in school for I could master any subject with perfect ease. I asked Ghuggi about his choice and he told me that he wanted to open a meat shop because of his love for cutting animals and hence, he was opting for Biology.

Unable to get any clarity, I decided to think for three minutes about my ultimate goal in life. If I had to become 'Father of Punjab'; I had to learn politics and if I had to learn politics, I also needed a good grip on history for there was nothing to learn from modern day politicians and good politics could only be mastered by understanding historic politicians like Chacha Nehru ji and his friends. Therefore, I opted for Political Science and History.

The classes were to start ten days after the admission process. Both of us returned to our village to enjoy the well-deserved and hard-earned ten days sabbatical but five days into my holidays, I got a letter from Sant Singh College that I had to appear for an interview with Principal Sir to get my admission confirmed. I was in seventh heaven because Ghuggi had not received any such letter, maybe they found him too substandard to be presented before Principal Sir ji!

God ji, Principal Sir at Sant Singh College was very different from our school Principal. Unlike our school Principal, he was neither fat nor bearded and even had a computer at his desk. As soon as I entered his room, he gave me well-deserved respect by asking if I wanted water. I wish I had accepted his offer because for next twenty minutes I was going to loose all the water of my testicles.

"So son, do you know why I have called you for this interview?"

"Yes uncle ji, you have called me to make sure that I join your college only and not any other big college in cities like Chandigarh and Ludhiana."

"And why do you think so?"

"Because I have always scored great marks in all my classes and was even the monitor of 10th A in Government Middle School, Dangar Khera."

"Oye *khotey*, I don't know all that but what I know for sure is that I can't give you admission in my college because your name will have bad influence on all the students, especially the girls."

"Why, sir ji?"

"As if you don't know. Tell me the meaning of your name."

"I don't know Sir ji but I believe it must be something very good." I thought it to be the most intelligent answer so as to confuse and distract him from the real meaning of my name.

"*Waheguru, Waheguru!* You don't even know the meaning of your name!"

"No sir, but please tell me if you know it." I thought it to be the most intelligent answer again because I was sure that he would feel shy to tell me the meaning of my name. Somehow, I was at my intelligent best that day.

"Look *kake*, I am not sure if you are old enough to know all this but at your age, I knew everything about it so I think I should tell you this." Saying that he took out an old tattered book named Debonair from his drawer and showed me a cloth-less picture of a smiling man lying beside a smiling woman.

"Do you know who these two people are?"

With one eye on him and the other eye on that picture, I replied with full confidence, "No sir." Somehow, that picture was making me very erotic in my *pyjama* but the presence of Principal Sir in that room was reducing that eroticism.

"They are husband and wife like your mummy ji and papa ji. They are looking so happy because they just performed what your name means. Now tell me, if I give you admission, especially the teachers and students would keep on thinking about this picture whenever they see you and no one would be able to focus on studies. I can't take this risk. Please take admission somewhere else."

"Sir ji, this is not a big worry. You can hide this picture in some bank or somewhere else so that no one else sees this and this way no one would think about it." God ji, as I told you, I was at my intelligent best that day.

"*Wahegure, Waheguru* this generation knows nothing. *Kake*, these pictures are available everywhere these days and it's not going to be of any help even if I hide this single picture."

"Then what do we do, sir ji?"

"The only solution is that I don't let you join this college. It will be good for everyone, especially you because then you can leave these boring studies and enjoy life in the village. I wish someone could guide me like this when I was young."

For a moment, I got so influenced by what he said that I thought of touching his feet for enlightening me with his wisdom but then the realization of not being able to become 'Father of Punjab' in future because of half education got me concerned.

"Sir ji, I agree to what you are saying and I would have loved to do that but I need to attend college to become father…"I stopped midway for I could not disclose what I wanted to become or he would also have decided to become the same thereby increasing unnecessary competition for me.

"Why don't you understand!!! We don't teach how to become father in our college. I order you to take admission somewhere else. Now get out."

"Sir ji, I will not get out until you confirm my admission," and I sat on the ground next to his feet holding the front left foot of his old cane chair.

Though he did not show it but he was a little angry at me for holding the foot of his chair because he kept shouting a lot of bad words at me for the next ten minutes. Finally, his vocabulary of bad words finished and he slapped me thrice but I still did not leave that chair.

Though I was ready for him to abuse and slap me for years without me leaving his chair, he got tired and finally decided to give me admission but on one condition – I was not supposed to tell anyone about that book in Principal Sir's room and the meaning of my name.

God ji, my life became very free when I joined college. There was no uniform and we were free to wear private clothes every day. We could leave periods without permission, we did not have to wait for recess to go to canteen, we could enjoy dirty shoes and long nails and lastly, we were free to indulge in watching beautiful girls. I was also happy because I also got blessed with a supporting friend in the form of Ghuggi. He used to pick me up from my home on his Yamaha RX 100 motorcycle which we used to park at Chacha Sweet House and catch the bus of Nagpal Travels to Abohar.

Though that bus did not accept 'student travel pass' but we still preferred that bus because unlike government buses which stopped only at bus stand of Abohar, it used to drop us exactly at the start of the College Road. Hand in hand, Ghuggi and I used to walk to the college on that beautiful and romantic road. Sometimes, on good weather days, we even used to sing a few songs like national anthem or our old school prayers.

We used to return by the government bus in the evening and Ghuggi used to drop me back home. I never paid Ghuggi for his services, but on a few rare occasions, when I earned some quick rupees by selling the old notebooks to Devi Dyal *kabadi*, I treated him to a *samosa* or a *gulab jamun* from Chacha Sweet House. Because of our different subjects, I used to meet Ghuggi only during English periods during college hours so I felt the need and requirement to make new friends but it turned out to be the most difficult thing to do. God ji, unlike my school where I first made illiterate friends and later, they got to know the meaning of my name, the college was full of literate students. In a matter of just a few hours on the first day of my college, my entire class knew the meaning of my name and by the second day, entire college including the peons and the canteen waiters were fully aware of the significance of my name.

The one major relief in the college was that though students teased me in tons, no one wrote my name on the college gate, walls or in the examination answer sheets. Moreover, I did not understand their teasing as most of them teased me in English. After researching for seven days, I found out someone who was also suffering like me and made him my first friend. His name was Mohit but everyone used to call him Patang because he was very thin and tall. Like me, he also hated his name but the only difference was that I hated my *pukka* name given by my mama ji and he hated his *kachha* name given to him by other students. His problem was not with the word *patang* but in the way people called his name.

'Cut the Patang', 'Fly the Patang', 'Hold the Patang tightly' or 'My Patang got torn' were the kind of dirty remarks which he faced every day. While I was short and could hide myself in the crowd to avoid being noticed all the time, he did not have that choice. He could be noticed and teased from a long range also. He was in my class so it was easy for me to propose him my friendship and in no time, we became very good friends. Be it sitting close to each other, sharing lunch boxes or visiting the bathrooms, we did everything together. Very soon we realized that like husband and wife, we could not get satisfaction from each other and hence, we needed more people in our group.

God ji, there were three more students in our class who could become our friends. Harjeet alias Nikka, Satwinder alias Mota and Harman alias Harman. While Harjeet got teased because of his short height and Satwinder's problem was his more than a hundred kilograms body, Harman was normal and had no physical, mental or nomenclature problem but he was also one of the targets because he was related to Satwinder. It so happened that Satwinder's mother married a man who was Harman's father's younger brother and in Punjab this kind of a relationship between Satwinder and Harman was considered at par with real brother. We were sure that Harman had no other path but to follow the footsteps of his brother when it came to friendships and we proved to be correct.

Initially, Mohit and I decided to convince Harjeet and Satwinder to become our best friends. Since it was not possible for Mohit - the tallest guy to bend every time and talk to the shortest guy Harjeet as it would have added another compliment hunchback or *kubba* to his illustrious name Patang, so I decided to entrap Harjeet while Mohit took it upon himself to negotiate with Satwinder and in a span of just three days, we had three more people in our group. In all this development, one strange thing happened - as the size of our group increased, teasing of our group members reduced. Who would have dared to tease a group, which consisted of the tallest, the fattest, the smallest, and the most intelligent student of class XI-A.

Life became even better because Satwinder and his brother Harman were from Abohar and used to come to college on a Luna and sometimes, I used to get a chance to sit my ass on that two-wheeler. Five of us became inseparable and life looked like a bed of sunflowers when a calamity struck our group. Harjeet failed in the class exams and since he became our junior, we had no option but to expel him from our group. Harjeet tried his best to convince us to retain him but we could not do anything. It was the time for us to tell him a goodbye. Once he left our group, his life became tough again as he got renamed as Nikka but our life was still the same because our group size at four was still big enough to reckon with.

God ji, as time flew by, the college absorbed me completely and I became corrupt. I was no more a decent student who used to ask 'may I come in' before entering the class and I became worse with time. I started sleeping on the last bench during the classes, became a participating member in the rumors about unmarried male and female teachers and to the embarrassment of my *sanskars*, I even started teasing girls.

God ji, modern day colleges are not like the *ashrams* of your era where you and your brothers stayed peacefully for years and learnt non-technical and easy subjects like archery, wrestling and a few *shlokas*. Colleges these days are very fast and furious, and the subjects are lakh times tougher. However, despite tough subjects, everyone in college wants to do everything except learning those subjects and I was no exception to this bug as I too picked up a lot of unwanted habits. It was easier for me to pick all the dirty habits except one. God ji, as you know that I am very handsome and smart but still teasing girls was the toughest and the most un-affordable pursuit that I tried to learn. Harman became my guru in this mission and introduced me to the art of teasing. He was just one year older than me in age but was years ahead in teasing as he had been doing that since his school weeks. While in the first year of my college, I just indulged in looking at girls or 'baking eyes alias *aankh sekna'*, it was in the second year when the real action started. It was not by intention that I fell for teasing but Harman deliberated it and he had reasons to do so. Despite knowing my below average teasing potential, he still continued his partnership with me until that un-fateful day of my 12th standard History board exam.

It was just one hour into the exam but being a good historian, I had already completed my exams and was waiting for Ghuggi to finish his Chemistry exam. God ji, as you know that I can't waste time, so in order to utilize my time, I went to the two- wheeler parking at the entrance of the college. I loved going there as seeing the scooters, motorcycles and mopeds entering and leaving the parking area used to give me eternal bliss. God ji, whatever I am going to tell you next is very painful and you need to read this with a heavy heart. It's embossed in my memory and to this day, I clearly remember that vehicle, a black colored Kinetic Honda. It was occupied by two not so young - not so old, not so fair - not so dark, not so beautiful- not so ugly girls with their heads and faces wrapped in their *dupattas*.

As soon as their Kinetic Honda reached near me, it stopped and the girl sitting in the back seat pinched my buttocks and sang, "*Munna, aaja meri gaari main baith ja, Aaja meri gaari main baith ja.*" They were fast enough to elope before I could even react to that attack of immorality on my self-respect. I was disturbed because that not so yankee – not so *desi* girl had called me *Munna* and sang a lewd song in the broad afternoon-light in the presence of the parking guy. I immediately ran to the canteen, found a vacant table, kept my head on that to pretend that I was sleeping and silently cried till my tears gave up. Finally, I got up, went to the bathroom, washed my face and decided never to tease a girl in my life ever again.

God ji, you would be happy to know that I never failed in any of the classes in college and in just five years, I finished my graduation. Some people say that it was because of my cheating skills, while others said it was because of the leniency of the Punjab State Education Board and Punjab University but if you ask me the real reason of my achievement, it was my 'anticipatory brain'.

While in school, I scored brilliant marks by studying and home-working hard but in college, I did not resort to any of these malpractices and devised a new strategy for success. My strategy was 'think how a teacher thinks'. God ji, teachers are also homo sapiens and like all homo sapiens, they are lazy. Just like their students, they also don't work hard throughout the year and have an addiction to procrastinate everything to the last hour. God ji, imagine a teacher who is married with a wife, has a few kids and a couple of parents to take care of. Imagine it's a day before the exam and he has not written the question paper. Imagine he also has pick his wife's salwar suit from the tailor, buy lollypops for his children from the confectionary shop, take his old parents to Gurudwara and purchase vegetables and fruits for food. With all this pressure and time crunch, how can he write the question paper unless he follows the path of his elders and steals questions from the previous year's question papers or from the guess paper. That's what I also did. Every year, though I did not care to buy my textbooks but without fail, I used to buy two most important books from Pee Kay Stationary Mart- Sartaj Guess Papers and Swan Old Question Papers. There used to be five speculative guess papers in Sartaj and ten actual papers from previous years in Swan.

Every year from 1st January to 1st March, I used to analyze those two books hours at a stretch to arrive at five questions per subject common to all those fifteen papers. It might look difficult to you but actually, it was very difficult. God ji, can you imagine someone going through two hundred twenty five questions per subject to find just five repetitive questions? The exercise was not simple and involved a lot of hard work. I kept on using this technique to wade through the tough exams of college. While others around me kept on failing not once or twice but again and again, I continued my winning spree and became a graduate.

God ji, unlike other classes where I used to get my mark sheet from the clerk adjacent to the Principal Sir's room, our college decided to have a function called 'convocation' to distribute us the 6"X 5" laminated certificates of B.A. Our local Magistrate ji was invited as the Chief Guest on the tented terrace of our college on a Monday morning to honor us with those certificates. It was a big day for all of us as we reached the college at 7 A.M. and that function continued until 2 P.M. While it was the happiest day of life for most of my classmates, it was the most disturbing public ceremony of my alive life.

As usual, I was sitting in the third row from the front surrounded by Ghuggi and Patang. Our Principal Sir was announcing the names and Magistrate ji was shaking hands with us and before giving the degrees. Finally, after a wait of many hours, my turn came but rather than announcing my name, Principal ji indicated to me to come to the stage. Though I got angry but I forgave him for this behavior and ran to the stage. I was on the verge of reaching Magistrate ji that Principal ji said,

"*Oye landu*, don't spoil the new carpet with your dirty shoes, remove those and come."

His guts were like never before. First, he used his fingers to call me and then he called me '*oye landu*', the way people called their servants in Dangar Khera.

I forgave him once more, removed my shoes and rushed to shake hand with magistrate ji but in that excitement forgot to check my socks.

"Principal ji, what kind of students do you have in your college? They don't even have basic etiquettes. I have never seen anyone wearing torn socks on the day of Convocation," Magistrate ji asked in the loudest possible voice to ensure that he was audible to everyone.

"What is your name, *kake*?" He asked before reading my name on the just received certificate in his hand.

"Fuck."

"I could not hear you, once again please."

"Fuck Singh." This time much louder, but not as loud as to reach the ears of the peons and the canteen staff.

"Oh, my *Ram!*" and he started wiping his sweated face.

"Oh, my *Ram!*" chorused all the students who had become active to the entire episode by now.

"Principal ji, how could you allow this kind of indecency in your college?"

"Shut up everyone! I will break your legs if you chorus anything now." Principal ji announced.

"I am not talking about their indecency but the indecency of this boy's name. Why didn't you do anything about it?"

"*Janab*, I tried my best but this boy held my chair so tightly that I had no other choice." Principal ji replied wiping his stressed face.

"Oh! I can understand now. Thank God, you relented or it would have taken you years to get a new chair issued from our bankrupt government. *Ha ha ha.*"

"*Ha ha ha*," Principal ji echoed.

Cybercafé - Day VI

The Search Of Needs

God ji, once I was done with my graduation, I got focused and I started searching for what I needed the most – money and wife. Money to achieve wife and wife to achieve fatherhood and thereby, taking my first step in becoming the Father of Punjab. You might be thinking that earning money and reproducing children for an intelligent, smart, handsome and horny man like me would have been the easiest thing in the world but believe me God ji, it was even tougher than you defeating the ten - faced Mr. Ravana in the 'Battle of Sri Lanka'.

God ji, there were three ways for me to earn the money - selling some portion of our agricultural land every year till my death, selling my buffaloes and other household stuff one by one each year or to get into a job. Given the freedom to choose, I would have definitely picked either of the first two options but the unintelligent demon named my papa ji did not let me exercise the easier ones and left me rein- less like a wild ox to search a job on my own.

Initially, I acted on the advice of the government employees of my village and started reading Rojgar Samachar but two months went by without me getting a single suitable job of my choice. All the jobs in that big newspaper had either written tests or some obscene percentages of marks as preconditions and I was not comfortable with either of those. I wanted a job where I could directly go for the interview, talk man to man or man to woman, impress the interviewing man or woman with my aura and make them beg me to accept the job.

God ji, thanks to the foresighted intelligence I have, I was not sitting idle while going through the government jobs of Rojgar Samachar but was also simultaneously analyzing and understanding the local private job market which made me realize that there was a desperate need for private companies to hire a damsel candidate like me. God ji, there were three very big conglomerates in Abohar – Abha Flour Mill, Sardar Cotton Factory and Lamp Oil Company. As usual, I had some near or distant relatives in all those companies and no sooner than I told them about my intention to work in their companies, they were up in the air to grab me. Within weeks of breaking off my dependence on Rojgar Samachar, I got my first interview call from Lamp Oil Company through Mutti.

God ji, Mutinder alias Mutti was the nephew of my papa ji's -wife's husband's -father in law's -cousin but despite such a distant relationship, he was closely associated with my family in terms of love and that's how I happened to approach him. He referred me to the owner of his company, Mr. Ramesh Garg for the post of Assistant Clerk. Mr. Ramesh Garg was no stranger to me or for that matter to anyone in Abohar. He was not only the owner of biggest vegetable oil company in the constituency but also the President of Dusshera Committee, Abohar and the biggest contributor to the *Ram Leela* fund every year. No Ravan had ever been burnt in the grounds of Higher Secondary School, Abohar on any Dusshera for the previous dozen years without his initiating the ignition. Though I had seen his photograph a few times in the local black & white newspaper, Abohar Tasvir, but as usual the printing quality of those photos was so bad that I was taken aback when I saw him for the first time from a close range in his huge office. He was not at all the way I had assumed him to be. Unlike his young, smart and youthful photos in the local newspaper, he was very old and very un-smart. Sitting at a distance of just three feet, that old man with round spectacles and cream *kurta payjama* started interviewing me in broken Hindi mixed with unbroken Punjabi.

"*Bolo!*"

"Sir ji, Mutti Uncle selected me for an interview with you for Assistant Clerk."

"How do you know Mutti?"

"Sir ji, his family and my family are related through my mother's family. Moreover, his land is also next door to ours."

"Which village?"

"Dangar Khera!"

"Oh! You are from Dangar Khera. Nowadays all villagers like you want to work in the cities. Why don't you work with your papa ji on his land?"

"Because my papa ji also does not work on the land. We have given it to a *bihari bhaiya* on contract."

"So sad! Entire young muscular energy of Punjab is getting wasted on music albums while *biharis* are enjoying our lands. Anyway, tell me where have you have worked till now?"

"I have worked as a monitor in class X-A and also, as the caretaker of buffaloes at home."

"We don't count that as work because everyone in Punjab does that at one point or the other in one's life. Have you ever worked in some factory or office?"

I was not able to tolerate his generalization. How could he say that everyone had done this at one point or the other? I could still digest his view about buffaloes but his idea about monitor hood was way below the belt. God ji, this was my first insulting experience in the corporate world and I did not how to react. Not able to find anything reaction-worthy, I gulped in that phlegm of emotional wound and replied,

"No, sir ji."

"*Behan ch*d*, Mutti. I told him very clearly that I only need experienced people but he sent you. I don't know where do I fit you?"

"Sir ji, I can do anything worth or not worth doing in your factory." I thought of showing him my hunger to convince him of my fitment for a suitable job in his company for I had heard from a lot of teachers in my college that starvation was the key to success in a job interview.

"I need a tempo driver to transport the oil. Can you do that?"

"Sir ji, that's the kind of work I have always dreamt of. I love driving so much that if you want, I am even willing to work without any salary."

"Good, in that case we will not give you any salary for the first three months but a lot of money after that if you perform well."

"I don't know how to thank you sir ji. Can I wash your feet or massage your legs?"

"Sure! But not today as I took bath in the morning, maybe some other day. Can you also give me your matric certificate so that we can apply for your driving license?"

God ji, I can't tell you how happy I was. First, the job of a driver and second, the chance to get a license. I had just started thanking you from the bottom of my pants when a sudden calamity struck.

"What is this? Your name is Fuck?"

"Sir ji, forget that name. You can call me by whatever name you want! Ramu, Shamu etc. I would love any name given by you." My hunger for job knew no bounds.

"Look *chottey*, I am not God that I can change your name overnight. Even if I call you by some other name, I will still not be able to cut others' tongues. Moreover, I have an old wife, Kanta and two young daughters, Garmi and Sardi. Who would marry them if the world gets to know that my driver's name is Fuck?"

"But your wife is already married and if you want, I can marry your daughter. After all, I am a young, futuristic *jat*."

"Why don't you understand? I have two daughters and not one. Moreover, I want them to be married to a *bania* and not a *jat*. Now before anyone gets to know your name, I want you to leave my office immediately. And for *Wahe guru's* sake, don't tell your name to anyone in my factory."

"Sir ji, I will die as an unmarried beggar on the streets of Abohar if I don't get this job. Please accept me before it's too late for both you and me."

"I like your confidence and your sense of logic but I can't hire you till the time you take rebirth with a different name. Now, will you leave or I take out my stick?"

God ji, this is one of the major disadvantages whenever a young man fights against an old one. Old people are always armed with walking sticks, which make them indestructible. I really wish that you had given the young people also something like that to carry.

Wasting no time, I rushed out of his office, his factory and my dream destination, and never looked back to appear in any other interview. Two months later, I got a chance to meet Sardara Singh of Sardar Cotton Factory located in the heart of Abohar.

God ji, Sardar Cotton Factory was a well-known factory in and around Abohar not for its size but because of its siren. It had a famous siren also known as *ghuggu* which used to blow thrice a day – morning, afternoon and night to indicate the beginning and end of shifts. However, that overly loud siren did not only indicate time to the factory workers but also to the entire city. Most of the people in Abohar were so dependent on *ghuggu* that they did not invest in a watch and used *ghuggu* as a benchmark to understand time.

So God ji, on one not so fine morning at the blow of the first *ghuggu* of the day, I reached the factory to meet its third generation owner.

"*Sat sri akal*, sir ji. I am interview in your factory for work." After the debacle in the first interview, I had decided to use every possible quality in me to impress the interviewer and this was the reason that I was speaking in flawless English.

"*Puttar*, I never went to college as my papa ji forced me to sit in this chair as soon as I failed in my 8th standard exams with good marks. Though I am fond of the way how young educated people like you speak great English but I am sorry, I cannot understand even a bit of it. Speak to me only in Punjabi."

"*Janab*, I want to work in your factory."

"What is it that you can do the best in my factory?"

I never expected him to ask such a complicated question at the launch of the interview itself. Despite thinking hard for a few minutes, I could not arrive at a suitable answer. Though I had known his factory since birth but I had never cared to know what exactly they did. The name was Cotton Factory so my brain suggested that they must be doing something with cotton but I could not think beyond that. I tried envisioning different options to use cotton but could not think of anything other than making mattresses and pillows. Although making pillows and mattresses were not un-interesting activities but I did not want to tell him that as my choice of work because I knew those two products only superficially from my experience of just sleeping on them. Had he started asking in-depth questions about those, I would not have been able to answer. Other than mattresses and pillows, the only thing that struck my huge brain was *ghuggu*. I said,

"I can blow *ghuggu*. Much louder and longer than the one we just heard."

"It's something that I like doing myself as it's the easiest work in this factory. I just need to press a button for that. Moreover, did you learn all this English to blow *ghuggu*?"

"Sir ji, you are getting old with each passing day. Don't you think you should pass on this responsibility to a dashing person like me?"

"I am just forty five and even at this age, I am much younger than you. How many large copper glasses of *lassi* can you drink at one go?"

"Uncle ji, with your blessings I can drink eight glasses even after having food." Though I had never drank more than six glasses but that was two years back on the *Baishakhi* day and I was sure that my capacity would have increased by at least one glass with each year of age.

"I can drink at least a dozen glasses anytime during the day," was his swift and proud response.

"*Behan ch*d!*" I could not control my excitement.

"Hmm, now you know that I am even younger than you. *Puttar*, I like you a lot because even eight glasses is not bad but the only work I have in my factory right now is for labor and illiterate people. I have no work for a flawless English speaker like you."

"*Malko*, I don't know any English. I just crammed that introductory line from one of my friends to impress you."

"*Sachhi?*"

"*Mucchi!*"

"In that case, I can hire you as a line worker. You can come from tomorrow morning. By the way, what's your name?"

Though I was super nervous answering his question but knowing his illiteracy level, I was confident that he will not be able to make out the meaning of my name.

"Fuck Singh."

"What is this name? I am sure it's not Punjabi. Is it Hindi or Urdu?"

Though I could have easily lied to him about the origin of my name but seeing the honesty in his eyes. I could not control my tongue and it moved on its own.

"*Janab*, it's an English name."

"ENGLISH!"

"Yes, uncle ji."

"Get out of my office. You lied to me that you don't know English. Leave aside knowing English, even your name is English. Thank you, *Wahe guru* for saving me from committing the crime of hiring an English man for the labor work."

"Have mercy on me, uncle ji!."

"You have mercy on me by leaving me with my uneducated labor. I am happy with them. Get out! But before leaving, tell me the meaning of your name at least."

I did not have a single drop of water in my testicles to explain him. With my muted voice, I gestured him the meaning of my name using my hands, fingers and tongue. Even before I could see his face or understand his reactions, I jumped out of the window behind his chair and came out of the factory.

"*Wahe guru*, thank you for saving me," was the last thing that I heard from that admirable man with the capacity of a dozen glasses of *lassi*.

Though within, I had decided not to appear in any further job interview but the fate had it otherwise. I got an interview offer from Abha Flour Mill as well. Had it not been for mummy ji, I would have never attended that interview but the prospect of getting flour at a discounted price motivated my mummy ji to motivate me to appear in that interview with full motivation. I appeared in that interview, answered all the questions related to flour and again got fired because of my name at a premature stage. It's not that the interviewer, Mr. Biggy Singh, who incidentally was also the Director of that mill disliked my name but he was childless.

God ji, while I had been wildly busy searching for a job, my papa ji in his greed to get enormous dowry had been figuring out ways to push me into some rich family. Though there were many rich families in our village but they all knew papa ji's lust for money. Therefore, papa ji decided to venture out to the neighboring villages to find a suitable match to pacify his monetary hunger. Surprisingly, he was not alone in this expedition as everyone from Sheela, Ramu to Nathhu of the neighboring *kirana* shop were supporting him. Maybe, he had offered them a share of the prize money. Though I had been without a job and had lost any hope for the same as well, papa ji was broadcasting that I was getting dozens of job offers from big companies in Ludhiana, Patiala and even Chandigarh. Though no one believed him with the kind of image he had, still one father of a below average beautiful girl from Badaing got influenced and decided to offer us free sweets at his home to tempt us to see his daughter.

God ji, Badaing is a small fertile village situated at a distance of fifty kilometers from the bank of river Satluj. I had neither heard of it nor been there ever. When mummy ji told me for the first time that we were going to visit Badaing to meet my future wife, I was both angry and excited. Angry at myself for having a poor general knowledge of Punjab and excited to get an opportunity to travel in a rented jeep. God ji, while my papa ji was a fly-licking miser but he was at his showy best when it came to sucking others money and that's how he planned my first meeting with Landi. Ironed clothes, washed shoes, starched turbans, gold chains and a jeep were a part of the plan to get the maximum profit out of Landi's papa ji. On the chosen day; all of us woke up early, got ready, ate breakfast, packed some food for the way, picked Cute and Giani ji, and started our journey to the place I was dreaming of calling my married home. While the journey was very comfortable in comparison to the bus, it was rain that added to the excitement. All of us were looking extra beautiful in our light clothes which got drenched and became translucent by the time we reached Landi's home.

Landi's home was not very difficult to find as her father Sardar Landa Singh had been the *sarpanch* of *panchayat* in the previous term and in Punjab, one is a celebrity if one ever becomes a *sarpanch* in one's lifetime. Her home was so impressive that from the front elevation itself, papa ji concluded that her father was priced at least more than a crore of rupees. To add to the glamour, there was one speed breaker each inside and outside that old house. No sooner than we entered, Landi's elder sister Kandi came out running bare foot to receive us. I was impressed the way she took us inside her well-lit and well-ventilated parental home and made us sit on a huge bed with a pigeon green bed sheet. Sardar Landa Singh entered the room with a wide roar and folded hands,

"*Sat sri akal*, Makhan *veer ji*. *Sat sri akal*, *behan ji*."

"*Sat sri akal*, Landa ji."

"I hope you did not get tired walking all the way from the entrance of this big house to this room."

"When you have an able son with hundreds of jobs, you don't walk but fly."

Though I was not able to understand why they were talking like that but I was able to notice one similarity in both of them. Both had their hands in *pyjama* pockets, chest bulging out of *kurta* and eyes completely red.

"When people have huge land and just two daughters, they don't need to work for others but they make others work for them."

"Everyone in Punjab has land but it's only the courageous few who are able to win jobs."

There was no change in the position of their hands but their respective chests were about to burst and so were their eyes.

"And those courageous few still search for the daughters of big landlords for marriage."

"And they get hundreds of such landlords to dispose of their daughters with those gems."

"Provided their fathers are also worth something in status and not just 30-40 acres type."

Till now, I was not able to understand anything. But now, I could at least make out that they were discussing something about land. What actually confused me was the over expansion of their chests and eyes. Somehow for the reasons only known to mummy ji, she interfered between those two men and said,

"What a beautiful home you have! I must tribute you for your color choice especially. Pink on the walls, black on the ceilings, red on the doors and even the green color of this bed sheet- you have got a true blue -blooded artistic taste."

"*Behan ji*, not only my home but my sperms are also beautiful. One look at my daughters and you will understand that."

"I completely agree, one look at Kandi and I was mesmerized. Now don't make us wait any further and call Landi."

"*Sardarni ji*, what is taking so long? *Behan ji* is getting desperate. Come fast and get Landi along." He shouted out aloud to invite his wife to show their daughter's face to us and then continued,

"*Behan ji,* this is the disadvantage of having such a big house. Even if they started hours back, they would still be on their way to reach this room."

"Had you had a jeep like me, you could have asked them to come in that." My papa ji could not sustain his silence any longer.

"Don't worry, we have a lot of time." Mummy ji interfered instantly and this time the reason of her interference was obvious. Papa ji in his moment of vigor had forgotten that the jeep was rented and we could not afford to let that secret out.

While everyone was still thinking about what to say next, two beautiful girls entered the room. One old, another young; one empty handed and the other with a tray full of *ladoos* and *burfis*. Though the older one was relatively much more beautiful but since she was old, I did not glance at her much and diverted my entire stare on the younger girl. Had it been any other day, I would have applied all my energies on eating *ladoos* and *burfis* and then thought about the girl but it was a rainy day with all of us being soaked to the nails so I focused only on that young girl. I looked at her thoroughly from top to bottom, spending more time on top than on bottom but she did not give me even one small look. As soon as she was done keeping the tray on the bed, she ran away without even doing the customary feet touching ceremony or insisting us to eat. Maybe, it was too improper for her to interact with her future-in-laws sitting in wet clothes on one of her beds.

As soon as she was out of sight, I took her out of my mind by putting her in my mummy ji's mind. I took my mouth near her right ear and said,

"Mummy ji, please marry me to this girl. She is much better than Cute."

Without even listening to what I said, mummy ji took her mouth near papa ji's left ear who in turn did the same to Giani ji and Cute. Before I could understand what was happening, papa ji got up, cuddled Landa Singh's chest in his chest and said,

"Starting this day, your daughter is our daughter."

Mummy ji also got up and repeated the same chest-cuddling thing with that old beautiful lady. I also wanted to participate in that cuddling exercise with that old lady but when I was getting up to get into the position for the same, she said,

"I am so thankful to you *behan ji*, but would you not like to see Landi before we finalize everything?"

"We just saw her and *kaka* also liked her. Isn't it, *kake*?"

I had no option but to go red in the face to indicate my liking. While on one hand, I was pushing my face to remain blush red and on the other, I was trying to hide my desperation to cuddle that old lady.

"When did you see her? She is still at the field collecting fodder for the buffaloes. She generally returns by this time. I don't know why she is late today."

"Then who was the one with the *ladoo* tray?"

"Oh! She is Channo. Our family maid's family daughter. If you like her, I can arrange for her marriage with your son but you will always have to keep a close watch on her. She commits so many stupid mistakes that I feel shameful even to mention those. Last evening, she added *lassi* instead of milk while preparing tea."

"*Hai hai*! *Lassi* instead of milk? We don't want our son to marry that kind of a girl. Who knows, tomorrow she might even add curd instead of milk!"

"Yes, *behan ji*. When I got married, I was so well trained by my mummy ji that I could cook food for hundreds of people blindfolded. You won't believe but I have given similar training to Landi."

"*Behan ji*, forget Channo. We are here to marry our son only to Landi. I am so blissful with whatever you told me that I am willing to say yes without even seeing her."

But I was not! Channo was definitely a piece apart and I could not forget her so easily. I elbowed mummy ji to indicate my choice but she was in no mood to understand my delicate signal.

"Channo, can you go and do the fodder and send Landi…" That old beautiful lady hadn't even exited all the words from her mouth when an old, ugly, insubstantial, breast less, bottom less girl with a mud sack on her head entered the room. In my mind, I was sure that she was either Channo's maid or some beggar in the need of a maid's job.

"*Burfi*!!!" She threw her mud sack on the ground, sat on the knees and started eating the milky white *burfi* with her coal black hands which had inexplicable dark nails.

"Eat, my Landi, eat. You must be hungry after working for so long with the buffaloes," that old lady was speaking her heart out while moving her lovely hands in that un-lovely girl's dusty hair.

"She is so hard working. I am sure even on the day of her wedding, she would not skip foddering the buffaloes," Landa Singh finally uttered those words to break the monopoly of the ladies who had been talking for a while now.

"And she is so good looking also. A perfect combination of beauty and hard working hands," that old lady supported her husband.

"We like the girl. Let's quickly fix the date of the wedding," my papa ji supported both of them by putting a one-rupee coin in Landi's hand. He took this decision without any inflow or outflow of whispers like it happened during Channo's selection. Before I could show any signs of resistance, everyone except me and Landi started hugging everyone else.

"*Veer ji*, what is your name?" Finally, Landi opened her dried white lips and asked her first question using her off-white colored tongue.

"Landi he is not your *veer ji*. You are getting married to him. Call him something else," her beautiful mummy ji was all ears to what she was saying.

"Something else like? Can I call him *Oye*?"

"Yes, that's like my intelligent Landi."

"*Oye*, what is your name?" She again asked using her off white tongue but this time looking hungrily at my wet body. The color of her tongue and the water level of my skin was all that was required to ignite a passion of love between us. In no time, I forgot everything that had been taught to me by my family and friends about hiding my name till my marriage cards got printed and I said,

"My name is Fuck Singh Brar."

"What a tasty name! I love it very much ji." I was not dumb enough to understand what she meant. She wanted to confess her love for my body but was using 'my name' as a disguise for that.

"*Kake*, is it Gulshan or Fuck?" Her beautiful mummy ji finally asked me something with her beautiful voice using very beautiful expressions.

I could not understand the relation between Gulshan and Fuck. Those two names neither rhymed nor meant the same but if she was asking, then there must have been some great reason because she was beautiful and beautiful girls are never wrong.

"Aunty ji , f you like Gulshan; call me Gulshan itself but at least call me. For the last one hour, you haven't spoken to me even once."

Till this day, I don't know how I got the courage to talk so romantically to her. Maybe, it was the effect of the wetness that had seeped into the core of my body.

"If that's the case, I will call you Fukka Singh. It's simple and healthy but I don't know why your neighbor, Nandi Aunty told me your name is Gulshan."

I looked at Cute and she looked at me, then both of us looked at each other. I understood her signal. She had asked her neighbor, Nandi Aunty, to lie about my name to get me married to one of her relatives. I did not mind her lying to Nandi Aunty but what rubbed me wrong way was the choice of name. How could she even think of naming such a handsome man like me as Gulshan? With age, it was not only Cute's beauty but her intelligence also that was becoming extinct.

"Really a very spiritual name like our *guru*, *Baba* Duck Singh ji. Its meaning must also be good. *Kake*, what is the meaning of your name?

"It's the English word for *thoka-thoki*."

By the time I opened my eyes, everyone except Landi had covered their ears with their hands. While everyone had a worried look, Landi had a big smile on her dry lips and then she uttered her last few words to me,

"I know what it means. It's really a very tasty name."

Though Landa Uncle did not hear what she said but he could not tolerate her smile. He got up, slapped her and took her out of that room. His beautiful wife started crying and apologizing,

"I have never seen my *sardar ji* this angry in the last three years that we have been searching a groom for Landi. I suggest you to leave our big home before he gets his hockey stick and starts beating everyone around. Don't take my words lightly because he has played hockey at a national level."

"National hockey player!" all of us exclaimed in joy.

"Yes, that's why he got to marry such a beautiful girl like me."

Without wasting any further time, we escaped from their home before the national hockey player could return. However, just then, I experienced one of the most beautiful moments of my life when Landi's mummy ji took me in her arms and wished me a long life. I had only one feeling when I was in her arms- the feeling of anger at my papa ji for not forcing me to become a hockey player. While all of us were sad because of our own reasons, it was papa ji who was the saddest as he had unnecessarily lost one rupee to Landi.

God ji, the search for my wife continued for another eighteen months and I met four more rich girls who were more than eager to marry me but their respective papa ji and mummy ji did not agree. While three of them refused to marry their daughters because of my name, the papa ji of the fourth one because of his deafness did not have any bias against my name. My relationship with his daughter was almost on the verge of being converted to marriage but at the last moment, he disclosed that he was bankrupt as he had spent his entire wealth on the treatment of his two sons and three daughters who were also deaf. I tried a lot to convince my papa ji but he could not tolerate giving away his son with an English name in charity and that's how I missed my only hope.

With time, everyone involved in my wife search got fatigued because of the repeated rejections. To my dismay, my own sister and her husband also changed their colors and asked me to find a wife myself.

Cybercafé Day - VII

Canada - The Foundation Stone Of My Suicide

God ji, after no success in either marriage or job endeavors, I started focusing on my family business. For the next two years, I took care of buffalo-ing and farming 24 x 7. With my passion and hard work, I took the business to the newer heights. In a short span, I achieved tremendous success in both buffalo-ing and farming. In those two years, the number of our buffaloes increased from six to eight as I promoted free sex in the stable. On farming front, I along with Bayer pesticides and *desi* fertilisers co-produced three successful harvests.

God ji, you have made Punjabi men very complicated; the more success they achieve, the more unsuccessful they feel and that's what happened to me as well. At an age, when I had everything what others could not even dare to dream like a *ghaint* personality, B.A. third class degree, eight buffaloes and thirty acres of papa ji's land, I still felt something to be scarce in me and it did not take me long to realize what it was.

It so happened that one early morning while working in the field, I felt the urge of deep sleep. While I should have controlled myself for some time and then gone home for sleeping, I did not do that. Nobody would have appreciated me sleeping while all of them were working. Therefore, I approached the base of the peepal tree in the eastern corner of our field; lied down with my arms folded under my head, closed my eyes and started dreaming. Everything till then was as per those old stories of my school text books in which a shepherd sleeps under a tree and some angel visits his dream to guide him on what to do in his life. However, I was not a shepherd but a farmer or more precisely a landlord and what happened to me was little different.

I kept on sleeping till late in the noon and tried hard to dream but could not dream even a bit because I did not have much experience of day dreaming. I might have continued sleeping like that for another few days but my fate and Miss. Maniari did not let that happen. God ji, Miss. Maniari was the pet pigeon of our neighbor Nathhu, the CEO of Nathhu Kirana Store. Every evening Nathhu used to un-cage her for her daily flight exercise which kept her young, healthy and full of vitality. She knew me very well not just because we were neighbors but because of her culinary interests in me. I used to feed her fifty-sixty grains every week without fail, which she used to eat very passionately.

That evening when I was in deep sleep, she happened to surpass our field during her exercise flight and while doing so she noticed me. She got perturbed and just like my insensitive mummy ji, she did not think twice before waking me up from that beautiful, un-dreamy sleep. However, unlike mummy ji, she did not use the slurs of her tongue but the charm of her beak to wake me up.

First, she bit me on the center forward of my beard, then on my right ear and when I did not relent, she beaked me hard on my eyes. Left eye, right eye, left eye, right eye and so on until I gave up my sleep and the first thing that I noticed after waking up was horrific. She had blood all over her beak, which was of the same red color as my blood. Even a fool could have understood that she had beaked that blood out of my eyes and I ran towards the village clinic. As soon as I reached there, I saw Doctor Subroto leaving for his home and from his body language I was sure that he was leaving early because he was in a mood to tight his wife Ms. Uttiya.

"Doctor ji, for the next five minutes, please forget your wife and look into my eyes instead."

I knew that it was a difficult demand because when a doctor had a fair wife like Ms. Uttiya, he couldn't think of taking care of anyone else but still, he obliged. He asked me to jump inside the clinic from the window as he had already locked the door and opening the door would have wasted five minutes. He followed me and jumped, and both of us were alone in that deserted clinic looking into each other's eyes. Though I looked into his eyes, he moved his eyes back and forth from my face to his golden watch. It felt as if time had stood still and five minutes elapsed even before I could even realize. Doctor Subroto got ready to leave and I begged,

"Where are you going, Doctor ji?"

"You asked me to look into your eyes for five minutes and I did that. I have to go now."

"But you have not put any eye drop in my eyes?"

"Look *sordar ji*, this village is poor and this clinic is even poorer. I don't have medicines for basic ailments like snake bites, dog bites, cow bites or pig bites and you want to enjoy eye drops. There are no eye drops in our stock. If you want, I can put cough syrup in your eyes."

"Doctor ji, look into my eyes. I am not asking eye drops for enjoyment sake but for treatment as I have been bitten by a lady pigeon."

"It's not just pigeon but I feel that you have been bitten by something else, that too in your brain. I don't see anything wrong with your eyes and I can't suggest any cure. However, if you still feel that you need treatment, follow your other village brethren and go to Canada or Australia to get the treatment done from good doctors there."

Doctor ji's nonsense was getting too much for me to tolerate. Without even saying thanks, I jumped out of the window and came home, but his words kept haunting me. There were just a few bites from a tiny creature, Miss. Maniari and our big country could not even treat me for that. Leave aside the treatment, the problem was that one of the best doctors of the country could not even identify my malfunction after staring into my eyes for five long minutes. For next one and a half night, I kept on thinking and did not sleep even a bit. I got up from my bed in the second half of the second night, went to the main sleeping room where papa ji and mummy ji were sleeping, woke them up and said,

"I don't want to remain incomplete anymore. I have decided to export me and my life from the ill-treatment of this country to a better world. I am going to Canada."

I returned to my bed, slept peacefully and never looked back again.

My experience of Canada was like motherhood. It started with pain, got worse along the way and ended with unbearable pain but all through I kept on thinking that it was the best thing to have happened to me. When I decided to transport myself to Canada, I realized that I could not just catch an aero plane and commute there, the way I did from Dangar Khera to Abohar because entry into Canada was filtered through a filter paper called visa. Moreover, Canadian government did not give visa to anyone and everyone who desired that but only to those people who had a book called Passport.

I consulted my mama ji and he told me that the first step in the process was to find out a reliable agent and I had to do that as quickly as possible. I started researching hard and in one week found out the best advisor for Canada in our village, Malla Singh S/o Sardar Palla Singh. He had won the Canadian visa and was leaving for Canada in twenty hours, forty minutes and ten seconds. I went to meet him in the late morning hours but he was still asleep as it was night-time in Canada and he was rehearsing for that. He looked beautiful and a pseudo foreigner in his sleep. Though I had no credentials to disturb him but I still challenged his sleep and woke him up. He woke up, organized his unorganized hair, tore a piece of cloth from his white bed sheet, wrote a name, phone number, address on that sheet, gave it to me and went back to sleep again. Though I was desperate to talk to him but in that helpless situation, I had no option but to leave.

Since he was leaving Punjab forever, his Punjabi had become really bad. It took me that entire leftover day to understand what he had written on that piece of bed sheet.

'Subedar Gupreet Singh (Retired),

Room No. 105,

Hotel Grand Look, Bathinda 0185-22378'

"Hello ji."

"Hello ji."

"I said Hello."

"Yes, I heard Hello."

I had never initiated a conversation on phone. I got physically and mentally challenged when a young, sweet sounding girl picked up the phone call meant for Subedar Gurpreet Singh Ji.

"Can I talk to your papa ji?"

"Why? Do you want to ask him for my hand in marriage?"

Though I got a baby orgasm but I was shocked and stunned. How could the daughter of a retired

Subedar talk this unintelligent. First, she did not ask me if I was married or not; second, she had not checked if I was younger or older than her and third, she had not even bothered if I had an elder sister or a brother to be married before me.

"Why have you become silent like a Hero Honda silencer? Did some snake bite you?"

"I want to meet him?"

"Oye, who are you and why do you want to meet him?"

"I am Fuck, a smart, young man with a B.A. degree. My papa ji is Sardar Makhan Singh and he has nine buffaloes and thirty acres …"

"Oye, shut up! Switch off your radio. You sound irritating like a mosquito but I am still talking to you because I like your name. Tell me, what is the meaning of Fuukk?"

Though I got my second baby orgasm, I got upset because she wanted to know more about my name than about me. Despite trying, I could not press the protruded button on the receiver of my phone to disconnect the call because her father was indispensable to me.

"It does not mean anything, it's just for style. Now, can I talk to your papa ji?"

"As if I care? Go to my home and talk to him for the rest of your life but please leave me now."

"What is your address?"

"*Accha,* now you need that also? Anyway, it's the first home on the left after the Government Primary School, Bulluana. Ask anyone about Bharawan *masi's* residence."

I did not talk any further as I was sufficiently embarrassed by then. I immediately pressed the protruded button and got ready for Bulluana.

I reached Bulluana by noon. It was around a hundred kilometers from Dangar Khera's bus stand. Papa ji gave me thirty rupees for the bus tickets and recorded it in a new notebook exclusively dedicated to my Canada trip. Bulluana appeared bigger than my village because it took me twenty minutes to reach *masi's* home from the bus stand while it used to take me just ten minutes to reach my home from bus stand in Dangar Khera. It was a small home and had only two people sitting in an open courtyard - an old uncle ji who was sitting on a charpoy and an old aunty ji who was squatting on a stool, both looking away from each other. Aunty ji was looking in the direction of the two small rooms and uncle ji was looking towards the main door. The door was unlatched and I couldn't hear any dog bark. I opened the door and went to uncle ji.

"Subedar ji?" I asked hesitantly as that old, junk looking uncle ji was nowhere close to the sleek, smart image of the Canadian agent that I had pictured in my mind.

"Yes."

"*Sat sri akal,* I am Fuck and I want to go to Canada."

The word Canada added a sudden excitement to the household. Old uncle ji became alert and the old aunty ji changed her direction and was looking at me now.

"Oh! Canada, the country where the postal stamps have the picture of a queen or a leaf. But why do you want to go to Canada?"

"One day when I was sleeping in my farmland in Dangar Khera, Ms. Maniari attacked me and damaged my eyes. Hence Doctor Subroto ji advised me to go to Canada for my eye treatment. That's why I want to go there."

Both of them looked happy and impressed. I was sure that I had convinced them to get me a visa which in turn made me happy.

"Please take us along, our eyes are also not too good and we also need treatment."

"Why are you making fun of me? You are the king of Canada. You can go there whenever you want."

Though he was not a king but I still addressed him as 'The King of Canada' because I wanted to boost his testosterones to make him active and arrange my visa as soon as possible.

"I am delighted that you came to our home today, but I am really sorry for your mummy ji who would keep on waiting for you to return from Canada and one day even die in your absence," aunty ji first opened her lips, said all those words and then opened her eyes and started crying.

"*Puttar,* you need to leave immediately. I will kill you if my wife sheds one more tear." In no time, uncle ji's facial expression changed from sweet smile to wild anger.

"I don't have a problem in getting killed but please get me a visa first. If you don't entertain me, who will get me the visa?"

"Ask *sarpanch ji*, MLA *sahib* or maybe Chief Minister ji. It's their job and not mine to get you the visa?"

"But Bharawan asked me to contact you."

"How dare you take my name without any respect? Shame on your upbringing, shame on your blood, shame on this young generation," aunty ji's tears evaporated and she started shouting. While I was concentrating on her loud words, she fetched a wooden *thapa* - the twin brother of a cricket bat used in villages for beating laundry clothes and started beating me heartlessly.

Angry at my poor upbringing and my useless blood, I sprinted out of their home and went straight to the P.C.O. at Bulluana bus stand.

"0185-22378"

"Hello ji."

"Hello ji."

"Haan! Who, Fuukk?"

"How do you know it's me?" Her sweet voice had done it again. I happily consumed my anger inside me and started enjoying baby orgasms.

"Bitti never forgets the voice she hears once. Moreover, in your case I remember you because I like your name very much."

"Who's Bitti?"

"I, Bitti. Who else? *Oye* Fuukk, leave all that. Can I ask you something?"

"Ask?"

"How many times have you thought about me since morning?"

"2.40"

"What?"

"Bitti, its already Rs.2.40 on the red P.C.O. monitor and I just have nineteen rupees with me. I called you to let you know that your name is not Bharawan, but I guess you already know that. However, since you did not know your correct name in the morning, I got beaten up by your mummy ji. What do I do now? I am sure that your papa ji will not get me visa now."

"What visa?"

"Canadian visa."

"Why?"

"It's a long story but I will explain you in short. My eyes have been bitten by Ms. Maniari and I need to go to Canada for my treatment."

"Then you must be looking bloody eyed like Sunny Deol *veer ji* in Ghatak. I like that look."

"3.60! Bitti, it's Rs.3.60 now. I am worried as I am not as rich as Sunny Deol ji. I am going to press this protruded button."

"Oye, Fuck, wait. Shall I tell you something?"

"Yes, but fast." Though my ears were listening to her, my eyes were continuously tracking the red monitor above the phone. After every 180 seconds, it was adding up Rs.1.20. I never knew that P.C.O. was such a lucrative business where people talked their money out so fast. It was worse than even gambling and I was sure that it was going to make people bankrupt in years to come.

"I don't know why did you meet my papa ji for visa. He is a retired post man and knows nothing but postal stamps."

"But he said that he is a Subedar."

"Yes, he is Sardar Subedar Singh Chawla. He doesn't know even a,b,c of visa. If you want visa then come to Grand Look Hotel, Bathinda. I work here and we have a retired Subedar who helps in getting visa."

"What? Then why did you invite me to Bulluana?"

"How would I know that you wanted to meet my papa ji for visa. Now stop barking and come to Grand Look."

"Hello, hello," I kept shouting but the phone only sounded toon, toon, toon. I checked the red monitor and to my happiness, the seconds had stopped moving. I unwillingly paid Rs.3.60 to the P.C.O. uncle ji and immediately jumped on to the bus to Bathinda.

Hotel Grand Look was not a complicated hotel to find. There was a big statue of your favorite disciple Hanuman Ji near the railway station and behind that statue was a lane which took me to Hotel Grand Look. I had never entered such an expensive looking hotel in my life but I still mustered the courage and went straight to the reception.

"Bitti?"

"Fuukk?"

"Haan."

"Haan."

"What is this? Why are you wearing a torn shirt? It's Bathinda and not your village! What will people say if they see you like this?"

"I wore a perfect shirt but it was torn by your mummy ji. It's not torn much. I can hide it." I folded the sleeves to hide the torn part near the cuffs.

"Now, please do as I say. Wait here for some time. I will give your name to Subedar ji and he will call you. Don't tell him that you know me. Else he will complain about it to our hotel manager."

"What complaint?"

"That one of my relatives looks like a beggar."

"But your papa ji looks like a sweeper. Then who looks like a beggar? Your mummy ji?"

"Shut up and sit there. If you want tea, drink it outside. It costs three rupees for a cup of tea inside this hotel. One more thing, the manager *sahib* is very strict. Use the road outside for urinating and don't dirty the hotel toilet."

I sat silently on a small sofa facing the reception and started revising Bitti's instructions. Grand Look was a different world altogether. The only trace of poverty in that world was either me or the turbaned man who was saluting every guest entering the hotel. *"Chal,* Subedar ji has called you."

She took me to a room with a steel door. She pressed some buttons and the door closed. I got panicked.

"Where is Subedar ji and why have you closed the door? If you want to loot me, I must tell you that I have only thirteen rupees in my pocket which I need for my bus ticket to Dangar Khera. However, if you insist, I can allow you to rob me a maximum of fifty paisa because the ticket costs twelve rupees and fifty paisa."

Before she could answer, the door opened and she pulled me out of that room and pushed me into another room which had 105 written outside. She left me there without even saying a single word.

"May I come in, Subedar Ji?"

"Come in, sit down and tell me what do you want."

Subedar ji was sitting behind a small table with two chairs - one for him and one for someone else. There was no trace of Canada in that room except a cloth banner in the shape of a red leaf with CANADDA written on it. His bed looked clumsy with papers scattered all around. He was a retired army person but had no glamour of army.

"I want to go to Canada."

"Legally or illegally?"

"Both."

"I am proud of you. In my ten years of ruling this business, this is the first time that someone has replied with so much of confidence. You are an ideal candidate for illegal immigration but that needs a lot of money. How much money do you have?"

"After taking care of ticket expenses, I have fifty paisa."

"I mean how much land do you have?"

"Thirty acres."

"Good, how many brothers and sisters are you?"

"Well, I have an elder sister. Her name is Cute and she was born on …"

"Shut up and please talk less. We don't have much time as I have to leave this room before the hotel guest comes in at 6 p.m. If you sell ten acres of your land to me, I will send you to Canada via Indonesia. I will arrange all the papers."

"Though ten acres is not much out of a total of 30 acres of our land but my papa ji is very stingy and he told me that he would not sell more than 2 acres of land for my trip."

"What a pity to have that kind of a papa! Anyway, when is he dying?"

"If I go by his looks, my estimate is that he will survive another ten to fifteen years. Moreover, he doesn't work in the fields any longer and may stretch up to twenty years also."

"Then come to me after twenty years and I will send you."

"Subedar ji...in twenty years, I will turn blind. You don't know my papa ji. He is very greedy and a big *harami*. You are such a great person. Please sponsor my visa and I will refund your entire money quickly. You are my only hope."

To reinforce my words, I started crying but it had no effect on him.

"Look, there are three ways to go to Canada. Point system, Family visa and *Kabootarbaji* - the illegal route. Point system is for hard working and English speaking people, family visa is for youngsters and *kabootarbaji* is for rich people. Since you don't qualify in any of the categories, I can't help you."

"But my eyes ...," even before I could complete my sentence, Subedar ji got up and started removing the CANADDA banner. I checked the big wall clock on my right side, it showed 5.50 P.M.

"Subedar ji, I know you are getting late but will you please enlighten me by telling some interesting things about Canada?"

"I am not your mama ji to do all that. Get lost now."

"Don't remind me of my mama ji, it hurts because he also lives in Canada."

"Who lives in Canada?" Subedar ji stopped cleaning his bed and gave me an excited look.

"My mama ji."

"Which mama ji?"

"The one who was reproduced by my *nana ji* and *nani ji*."

"*Oye nalayak*, why didn't you tell me this earlier? Let me calculate."

He started writing some numbers on a piece of paper and summed them up with a big calculator and kept on thinking for a few never-ending moments.

"If your mama ji sponsors you or gets you a job offer letter from Canada and if I manage a fake work certificate, you will be short of nine points. I can send you if you clear IELTS with a band score of nine. The good thing is that you don't need to worry about the cost, I will do that in just 2 acres of land."

I turned speechless; the world which had ended a few minutes back got reconstructed. I became emotional, authentic tears started rolling down my cheeks and with genuine feeling, I got up and touched his feet.

"I don't know if you gift CSD Canteen's whisky to your friends or not but you are the most helpful *fauji* I have seen in my life."

Emotions gave way to paper work. He gave me a lot of papers and also the estimated bill for his services. I had to complete all those documents and meet him again after two weeks. I came down and searched for Bitti but she was not to be seen. I waited for a few minutes but she did not come.

With one-half of my heart stuck on Bitti, I started working with the other half on my Canadian dream. My first two months got wasted in going to Sidana Academy, Abohar every day to prepare for IELTS which I finally cleared. Once through with IELTS, Subedar ji initiated the application of my trip but I never believed him because I did not receive any confirmation letter from Canada. I kept on waiting but nothing happened for the next eight months. I made it a habit to visit post office every Tuesday, Thursday and Saturday at 11 A.M. to check for a letter from Canada. I would also call Bitti every Monday, Wednesday and Friday at 10 A.M. to get an update on the status of my visa. Initially she used to be restless, take my calls at the first ring and very cutely say 'Fuukk' but with time, she turned lazy. Not only did she delay in taking my call to ninth or tenth ring but also changed my name to a slow, lazy, long 'Fuckkkkkkkkkkkkk'. In turn, I also took revenge and stopped my baby-orgasms. It continued like this and finally after eight months of waiting, on one of my morning trips to post office, I got a letter from Canadian High Commission. As soon as I got that letter, I rushed to the proud arms of mummy ji who in no time arranged 3.5 kilograms of *ladoos*. All our neighbors arrived at our home and each one ate 2-3 *ladoos* at least but did not give me any gift in return. While the celebration was still on, papa ji took me aside, snatched the sealed envelope from my hand and said in a philosophical tone,

"I am sure it's visa. Take this to Subedar ji tomorrow. Let him open this envelope and be the first one to read the good news."

Next morning, I reached Hotel Grand Look at 10 A.M. sharp. It was a Wednesday morning and Bitti was looking very tasty in a cream suit but I did not talk to her and went directly to the first floor. With the Canadian visa in my hand, she was out of my half heart as I could entrap dozens of girls like her. That was my fifth meeting with Subedar ji and I had become so used to him that I had even stopped asking 'May I come in?' while entering his room. I went straight to his seat and with a 'never seen before' confidence forcefully banged the letter on his table.

"Subedar ji, your dream has come true. I got this."

"What is this?"

"Visa, what else? You don't even know this?"

"But it's a sealed envelope. How do you know its visa?"

"Subedar ji, till now I was not sure if you ever went to CSD Canteen and helped your friends with whisky but now I have my doubt if you ever went to school also. Look at this; the stamp of Canadian High Commission, Chanakyapuri, New Delhi. They are not going to send me the wedding invitation of their Prime Minister. It has to be my visa."

"It's a waste of time to talk to a mindless monkey like you," he stressed a lot on the word monkey and opened that envelope. After a few moments, in a stressful tone he said,

"*Oye* donkey, it's not a visa but the letter from the embassy asking you to appear for an interview next week."

"Interview!" Though I was angry at him for using animalistic adjectives for me but at that moment I forgot the insult and started thinking about the next torture called interview.

"Yes, they want to interview you to make sure if you are good for their country or not."

"Of course, I am good. Not only good but I am even better than the best." My IELTS preparation had taught me that 'better' and 'the best' were the senior family members of 'good'.

"Don't worry, they will ask you some simple questions and you just have to answer those confidently. Now go back and start preparing for interview. One more thing, please wear a new pair of clothes for the interview. Don't go looking like this, dirty pig."

"Today is your day, Subedar ji. You can call me by any name you want. But remember, I will answer you the day I get my visa."

I took that letter and banged the door with full confidence and I left his room. This confidence was a little lesser than the 'never seen before' confidence with which I had banged the letter sometime back.

It was my living life's first interview and I was very hungry after a long journey. I reached Delhi by an overnight bus and rushed straight to Chanakyapuri from the Red Fort. To save time, I had worn my new white colored bush shirt, red colored jeans and pink turban the night before boarding the bus from Fazilka. I realized I was looking very young and smart because a lot of people were looking at my red hot look in awe and surprise. I reached Canadian Embassy at 6.30 in the morning.

God ji, within a few minutes of landing at the embassy, I made a very good friend - Mr. Ram Bihari Yadav. He was hard working man, trying even harder to clean the already clean road in front of the main gate of the embassy but was unable to get the 'mirror-like' cleanliness. Seeing him struggle helplessly like that, I could not control myself. I removed my blue rubber shoes, folded my jeans pant and snatched the broomstick from his hands. I dampened that broomstick from a nearby water tap and in no time made the road shine like a bridal trousseau. Mr. Yadav got very impressed with me and even offered me some water from his translucent, scratched water bottle. I drank that complete bottle but it still could not satisfy my hunger as I had not eaten anything since morning. I was happy and very hopeful that our friendship would last for ages but that myth got shattered when I requested Mr. Yadav to take me to his home or to some Gurudwara and offer me free food. Not only did he stop talking to me but he also turned a deaf ear to my words and immediately left for some other road. For the next two hours, I kept on searching for food on those neat roads of Chanakyapuri but could not find even a single grain of wheat or rice. Disappointed and hungry, I returned to the embassy and started getting ready for my interview.

To my amazement, a lot of people of different ages, colors and sizes had come for the interview. It felt as if entire India was commuting to Canada and that made me happy because that was an opportunity for me to become 'Father of Indians in Canada' in future. The security guard at the embassy honored me with serial number 'eleven' which meant that I was to be summoned for interview after an old uncle ji whose serial number was ten. While I was waiting for my turn, I did not waste time and kept on searching for some *langar* or food stall inside the embassy but could not find one. I failed to understand how people survived in the capital of India but it did not take me too long to figure that out. While I saw no one eating anything since morning, what I observed was that most of the people were carrying water bottles. Maybe, like Mr. Yadav, they all survived on water and no food. I had just started feeling excited at my enlightenment when my turn came for interview.

"Sat sri akal."

She did not respond.

"Good morning, madam ji."

There was a white lady sitting in front of me who was busy reading my papers. I was sure that she found my documents very interesting and impressive because she kept on reading those with utmost attention and did not even bother to reply to my impressive 'good morning' spoken in perfect English.

"What's your name?"

"Fuck Singh."

"*Ha ha ha*, pretty weird. I thought there was some typo in your papers. *Ha ha ha*."

I could not completely understand what she said. Weird was a new word for me but at that time I did not realize that I was going to hear that word every time I would tell my name to people in Canada.

"*Ha ha ha*," I also laughed but with a louder tone so as to give her an impression that I understood whatever she said.

"Pretty funny."

She was stuck at the word pretty. I closed my eyes and tried to decipher the word 'pretty' but could think of only one name which I had read many a times in Punjab Kesari's Thursday edition. I replied,

"No, Preity Zinta."

"Whatever, so why Canada?"

I did not know the meaning of 'whatever' but I understood the second half of her question and I also knew what to reply because Subedar ji had already prepared me to answer that question.

"I go to Canada and work very hard there. Canada happy, me happy."

"What kind of work will you do there?"

I was happy because now she was asking questions which Subedar ji had leaked to me beforehand. A lot of people had told me that the travel agents had connections with embassy staff but I never thought that those white people had fallen so low that they would leak their interview questions to those agents.

"I work in store, very hard. Canada happy, me happy."

"Who will take care of your expenses?"

"Fuck work hard at store for his expenses, *waisey* in emergency Fuck's uncle also there"

This was the only answer where I struggled a bit because I forgot the word 'otherwise' but I guess that white lady understood the word *'waisey'* as she did not ask me to translate it to English.

"What kind of a relationship do you share with your uncle?"

"He is my best uncle and I am his best nephew. He is the one who named me Fuck."

"Is it? I understand the closeness now. Ok, Mr. Fuck, *ha ha ha*. I am sorry, Mr. Singh. We will get back to you."

"Can I ask something?"

"We don't entertain questions. Better be fast."

"You have food? Eating *wala* food. I hungry. Mr. Yadav also no food."

"I am sorry Mr. Singh but this is High Commissioner's office and not a bistro! You can leave now."

"I do not sleep so no *bistar*, just food. If you no food then I find it outside. Bye. *Waheguru bhali kare.*"

While I moved on, she was still stuck on Preity Zinta as I could overhear her saying, "pretty crazy, what a nut."

As expected, I got my visa a few weeks after my stellar interview and my travel process became really fast after that. Within two weeks, I got my tickets, two big bags, a few colorful clothes and a lot of readymade under-wears which felt very uncomfortable and small in comparison to my erstwhile hand-stitched under-wears. God ji, it was not just me who was busy but everyone around me was busier than usual. While all my mornings and evenings were getting utilized in sleeping to adjust to the Canadian time, others remained awake to complete their tasks. Cute got absorbed in preparing two big charts with my name, address and destination to be pasted on my two bags, mummy ji spent most of her time in cooking to feed me my favorite food one last time and papa ji got occupied in opening bank accounts where I could deposit money directly from Canada without sending him money-orders. Not only my family but my *desi* neighbors also started taking undue interest in me and never missed an opportunity to give tips and suggestions on how to establish myself in Canada. I became the star of the village and youngsters started clinging to me with a lot of questions about 'How to go to Canada?' at every interaction.

Finally, the day arrived for which I was born. The day when I was to go to Canada. For some reason, papa ji, mummy ji and Cute decided to accompany me in a hired Maruti Van to Delhi Airport. Even after four of us sat comfortably and loaded my bags, there was some space in the taxi and I asked papa ji if we could also take one of our buffaloes along but he refused as taking one buffalo might have affected the sentiments of the remaining buffaloes. Somehow, the pain of loosing his younger son to Canada had made papa ji very sensitive. For a change, all three of them were talking to me in a nice manner but I knew that they were in deep pain within as they were jealous that I was going to fly in an aero plane, a feat which none of them had ever achieved in life.

We reached Delhi Airport at 11.09 P.M. and my flight was at 3 A.M. I unloaded my bags quickly from the taxi, pretended touching mummy ji's and papa ji's feet by actually touching their knees, saw mummy ji and Cute cry for six minutes and excitedly sprinted inside the airport. God ji, what I saw next was unimaginable; there was a flood inside the airport. I had never seen such a sea of people in my life except during *Maghi Mela* in Mukatsar. Everything was haywire. People were running here and there. It was just like Amritsar bus stand except that the conductors were not shouting, "Canada, Canada, Canada". I did not know what to do. While Subedar ji, mama ji and everyone else had imparted in me a lot of wisdom on how to survive in Canada, nobody had ever told me how to survive at Delhi Airport. Left with no option, I looked around. There were a lot of *sardar ji's* at the airport but all of them looked too well dressed to talk to me except one police constable who was standing peacefully at one end of the airport with untidy beard, broken shoes and half shirt out of his khaki trouser. I immediately rushed to the spot where he was enjoying in his standing position and grabbed him by his shoulder.

"Sardar Jaspal Singh."

I read his name written in white on his black name-tab pinned to his light khaki shirt.

"You, who?"

"*Sardar ji*, please tell me if it is a real airport because I can't see even a single aero plane?"

"Oye, aeroplanes are not like buses, they are very expensive so they are parked in tight security."

"But trains are also expensive and still they are easily available at stations. Why are they not parked in security?"

"Because unlike aero planes, they are big enough to take care of themselves."

With each passing moment, I was liking his intelligence. I wanted to talk to him about a lot of other things but I had paucity of time. Without talking further, I took out my ticket and begged him,

"This is my ticket. Please take me to the aero plane."

"I can't take you to the aero plane because this ticket is only for you and not for both of us."

"But you are police personnel! Why do you need a ticket? You can travel anywhere, eat from any shop, stay at any hotel without paying or buying any ticket."

"Kake, gone are those golden days of police empire. Nobody loves us these days to offer free services."

"In our village, we still do. Anyway, if not you, who will take me there?"

"Go there! The girl on that counter will help you. But before that, you need to get your bags x-rayed."

I started perspiring. Not only was I short of time to go to a hospital for x-ray but I did not have the money also.

"Sardar ji, I did not come in a bus but in a taxi from my village and on the way my entire family took adequate care of my bags. There was no accident so why do I take an x-ray? Moreover, papa ji has left, taking taxi back to Dangar Khera and auto drivers outside are big scoundrels. I can't do all this now. You need to take me to the aero plane without an x-ray. I want to tell you that I am very unhappy with you. Instead of helping me in this situation you are asking me to go to that semi naked girl. What kind of a Punjabi are you? If a *sardar* will not help another *sardar*, who else will? Remember *Waheguru* is watching all this!"

As usual, my two minutes speech motivated him so much that he himself took me to different counters and finally got the x-ray done at no cost. I did not lose much except the ghee box, *pinnis* and the pickle jar. Jaspal Singh told me that I was not allowed to take those to Canada. When I asked the reason for the same, he told me that it was to avoid rats in aero planes. I did not understand why was it a big deal even if there were a few rats in the aero plane. After all, most of us had grown seeing them everywhere from our kitchens to bedrooms. Even after repeated requests, when he did not allow me to carry those jars, I wrote my Dangar Khera address on a slip of paper and gave it to Jaspal Singh along with the jars and said,

"This pickle is a gift to you for your services but please post the ghee and *pinnis* to my home. Papa ji and Cute like these a lot and they would love to get them back."

Once through with the security inspection, I laid my ass on an uncomfortable chair and started observing different aero planes from the panes of a big hall. I kept on looking at those planes for next three hours and twenty minutes. My concentration got lost only when I heard my name. I heard my name on the loudspeaker; first, in English and then, in Hindi. Till then, I did not know that the Canadian visa had made me so famous that even the airport authorities knew my name. I was sure that I had won some lucky draw so I shouted, "I Fuck, I Fuck Singh."

A young man immediately escorted me to a bus which dropped me at the steps of an aero plane. Though they did not give me any lucky draw but the love with which they treated me was more than that. Not only did a suited man respectfully take me but he also gave me a completely royal treatment by taking me alone in a big bus. They did not charge me for that bus ticket also.

My plane journey was marred with a lot of controversies. First, the man standing at the ladder-step took my ticket, cut it into half and kept one portion with him. While it was not uncommon for ticket checkers in Punjab's buses also to cut the tickets into halves during their surprise checks but never ever in my life, I had got my ticket cut by a conductor before the start of the journey.

"You ticket checker or conductor?"

"I am sorry, I did not get you."

"What sorry? First, you cut ticket and now, sorry. First time you standing here?"

"Sir, what happened? Did I do anything wrong?"

"I Fuck. You just a worker. You cheat me. Give my ticket back."

"Sir, please don't use this language. We are getting late, please move."

"No tension, better late than penalty. If ticket checker comes in aero plane, then what I say?"

"What checker?"

"I no fool, I Fuck going Canada. Give my ticket back."

While he was not willing to give my ticket back, I snatched all the half tickets from his hand. Unable to locate my half ticket, I put all those in my pocket and laddered up the plane's door step.

He kept shouting something in English behind me. Since I was in a rush, I failed to listen and understand what he spoke.

Once I boarded, I rushed to get the window seat but to my dismay all of those were occupied. I could not accept my defeat so easily so I used my old *desi* bus trick. I went to the beautiful young aunty standing in the middle of the plane and requested,

"I Fuck. Only on window seat."

"What?"

"Driver drives aero plane. I Fuck, I vomit. I only window seat."

Though she looked modern but she was behaving like a maid. I later realized that she was actually a maid because she was carrying dozens of towels in her hand to wipe people off their dirt. I was sure that being a maid, she would not have cleared IELTS, I enacted to help her understand my point of view. First, I moved both my hands half circle clockwise and then anticlockwise to indicate driver and then, I pressed my throat with both my hands and took my tongue out to signify vomit but even then, she did not understand. Rather than taking me to the window seat, she ran towards the back door and got me a paper bag.

She was much smarter than my village bus conductors. Instead of giving me a window seat, she got me paper bag which I thought had orange candies to control my vomit. Then, she took me to a middle seat which had white females sitting on either side. I was too shy to sit between two women and I said,

"I shy Fuck, not between two girls."

"Sir, I request you to mind your language."

Though she was trying to be stern but she had a pleading voice so my *sanskars* advised me to settle the matter and sit peacefully. There was no virtue in fighting with a maid. While I was trying to calm down and forgive the airline staff, another controversy happened. I opened the paper bag and found no orange candies in it. It was just an empty bag. I could not tolerate such an insult.

"Cheating, cheating," I stood up while shouting.

That lady who was closing the overhead bins left it midway and came running towards me.

"What happened, sir?"

"Look at this! No *santara* toffee, only empty bag."

"Excuse me, sir?"

I pushed her aside and went to the aisle. I was not going to tolerate their tyranny anymore. It was my day to fight the injustices and oppressions of the aero plane staff; the way Mr. Bapu Gandhi ji had done hundreds of years back against the oppression of the train staff in South Africa.

"Brothers and sisters."

I shouted at the maximum possible pitch of my voice.

"I Fuck, educated village man going Canada. I *desi* but not fool. Aero plane boys and girls thief. First, ticket cutting at entry so I pay again if checker comes and now empty bag, no orange toffee inside. When I ask they tell sorry and excuse me. This not good. People I know you busy so no noise but I make noise. It does not mean that I no busy, I busy but I still fight like Bhagat Singh ji's younger brother. White people, you not know Bhagat Singh so I give his introduction. Bhagat Singh is a *shaheed*. He killed himself fight against whites. Not you whites but those old bad whites. You white, good white."

While giving my sermon, first I tore the paper bag in front of them to show that there was no candy inside and then I took out those half tickets from my pocket. Before I could distribute their half tickets among them, the same man who was at the entrance rushed to me,

"Sir, please give these tickets back to me."

"If you have liver, take these from my hand."

As soon as he brought his hand forward to collect those tickets, I held his hand and gave him a big jerk with a quick twist and he fell on the ground. I gave him three kicks on his chest as well while he was trying to get up. Finally, I threw those half tickets on his face and went to my seat. The two white ladies on my sides were looking fearfully impressed with me and I thanked them for not letting anyone else sit on my seat. While I was trying to settle in that seat, four of their employees came rushing towards me. One of them who looked older and intelligent said,

"Sir, we are sorry for any misunderstanding but I request you to keep restraint now. One more act of misbehavior and we will be left with no option but to hand you over to the airport authority."

"Good, you talk good." I liked the way he spoke the word 'sorry' and so, I complimented him on his English.

"Thank you sir, let me know if I can do anything but no more foul language with my staff, please."

"I corner seat, I vomit."

He was the only sensitive staff. He understood my pain and asked one of the girls to escort me to the corner seat in the last row. That girl was very intelligent. Not only did she make me sit but also tied a belt around me so that I did not run away. While leaving, she also gave me a paper bag and to my surprise, that was empty too. Though I had the energy to fight all over again but I had lost all hopes in them. I relaxed on my seat looking through the window and peacefully watched the land become cloud and then water and then land again. After a journey which involved many hours of sleep, a few trips to the neighboring toilet and a few boxes of good looking but bad tasting food, I finally felt a jerk, a few minutes after which the plane stopped. Despite having spent so many hours in the plane, I was still not content. After all, the flying hunger of so many years could not be satisfied in a single journey. I wanted to fly more but I did not have the money to buy any more tickets. While I was cursing my fate for having such a stingy father, I hit upon a brilliant idea - an idea which my classmates and I had practiced while traveling in trains without tickets to Bathinda. I looked around and saw everyone busy taking their bags out. I made perfect use of that opportunity and sneaked into the toilet. Courtesy my smart brain, I knew that the plane would be flying again in a few hours and I would have to just remain seated in the toilet till then. One great quality of the plane was that even the toilets were air conditioned so I could comfortably spend not only a few hours but even my entire youth there. It had been just a few minutes in that comfortable enclosure that someone started knocking on the door. First, I ignored the knocks thinking those to be from someone like me who also wanted refuge in the toilet but when it persisted, I had no option but to open the door. One of the lady staff standing there asked me nervously, "Is everything fine, sir?"

"Why fine? I did no wrong. Aero plane not started fly. I no pay fine."

Though I knew that I was being fined correctly for hiding in the toilet with an intention to travel without ticket but the plane had not started flying till then. Hence, I replied in a confident, loud voice to scare that girl and that's exactly what happened. She said nothing but sorry and I happily exited out of that plane without paying any fine. With a ten rupee note in the right pocket of my jeans, a lot of English in the right side of my brain and a lot of dreams in my right heart, I landed on a rainy day in Vancouver, the city of sixty thousand dogs and one lac trees.

God ji, first you created this beautiful earth, thank you very much for that. Then, you created beautiful countries, thank you very much for that too. Once you were done with all this, you created beautiful people, thank you very much even for that. I am sure by then you got so tired with all the creation business that you authorized those beautiful people to create new generations of further beautiful people on their own, thank you very much for that authorization also. But then you committed a big mistake, you gave the right to decide the names of the future generation to the older generation and that's how everything got scary. Though I knew all this in Dangar Khera itself but I realized its full magnitude when I reached Vancouver. Not just one or two but the entire city from the musician begging at the Robson Street to the crew members of the English film shooting at Vancouver Public Library knew in intimate details, the meaning of my name. From the moment, the lady at the immigration counter asked my name to my first interaction with most of the Canadians, my experiences were nothing but embarrassments with each incident increasing my urge to commit suicide.

God ji, on this second-last day of my life I don't want to write much about that city as there are no notable incidents from my Vancouver trip that would suit your taste of reading. I stayed there for nine months but those nine months were tougher and painful than the nine months preceding my birth and the only person responsible for all this was my mama ji. First, he gave me an unsuitable name for Canada and then, he invited me there. God ji, you and I share one common pain - the pain of having a cruel mama ji. While you killed your *mama* Kans before he could kill you, I am not that smart and I am killing myself years before my mama ji dies under the weight of his sins. God ji, after what I went through in Vancouver, I could have still been happy had my objective of getting my eyes cured been fulfilled but that never happened. Leave aside eye hospital, mama ji never took any personal interest in me and from the first day itself, assigned me to Sary. Though she also laughed at my name and ignored me initially but with time, she became my guide and started taking me out but on one condition, I was to change my name to Funk while going out with her. I accepted her demand of being Fuck at home and Funk outside as it was only a difference of one alphabet. At times when I missed my real name in public, I used to introduce myself as Fuck but with an accented 'c' which sounded more like 'n'. Sary took me to Stanley Park, Robinson Street, Grouse Mountain, China Town, Art Gallery and The Aquarium but the place which I liked the most was Punjabi Market close to 50th Avenue. I liked going there not only for eating an eleven dollar dinner buffet at All India Sweets and Restaurant but also to have a peek at the Punjabi village girls getting the threading of thick brows at Kohli's Mastercut or buying the clothes at Crossover Bollywood Se and Guru Bazaar Sarees &

Fabrics. Sary had a lot of friends; girls and boys, black and white but I could never become best friends with them because they lacked sophistication and sanitation. They had bad teeth, bad hair and above all, bad skin. Most of them were so ashamed of showing their real skin that they painted their skins with drawings; they even had a very funny name for those drawings called tattoo. Initially, I advised a lot of her friends to oil their hair every Sunday to retain the black color but they laughed at me without realizing that having white hair at that young age was nothing less than a sin. With time, I stopped advising them because there was no use of that on their deaf ears. Other than their sanitation and hygiene problems, they were cheerful. They laughed at everything. Even at my new name, Funk.

    Sary was a good guide. Other than taking me to tourist attractions, she also took me to night discos at Davie Street and Granville Street. However, I stopped going there once I saw a man kissing another man at Granville Street because I could not digest that happening to me some day. Though I had my *sanskars* intact and I would have still compromised those a bit if a neat and clean Punjabi girl would have tried to kiss me in a closed room but a man kissing me and that too in the open air, was very disgusting to even imagine. Going there at night was putting myself in a vulnerable situation as no one, including Sary could save a smart man like me from those kisses.

Though she took me around Vancouver a lot of times but she never took me to an Eye Care Centre. She told me that she would take me to Eye Hospital of University of British Columbia the day she met me at the airport but as time passed, she refused to take me there as she felt that my eyes were the most healthy eyes on this earth.

God ji, it's not that everything was bad in Vancouver. I liked the clean roads, green parks, internet and air-conditioners at homes, and occasional snowfall. Among humans, I liked Chinese people the most as they never laughed at me because I never spoke to them.

God ji, my initial few days in Vancouver were good because most of the time, I used to be at home or go out with Sary for sightseeing but with time, it became intolerable. First, it was my papa ji who was after mama ji's life to get me some work and earn for him and then it was mama ji himself who pushed me to take some job. While I liked the police uniform of 'Vancouver Police Department (VPD)' and wanted to join that, mama ji made me work as a shop assistant. For five months, one week and three days I worked at mama ji's friend's shop 'Best Antique Shop' at South Granville on W 13th Avenue but I left that because of two reasons. First reason was the identity card hanging around my neck with a big Fuck written in capital letters on both the sides and whoever came to that shop asked more about Fuck and less about those so called show pieces. Irritated, I even threw that card in False Creek and pretended to have lost that but then I was issued a new card along with a warning of salary cut in the situation of any subsequent loss. Second and the foremost reason for leaving the job was my rock solid character. God ji, I won't say that I have never lied in my life but I have never lied to poor people with an intention to loot them. However, at Best Antique Shop, I was being forced to do that. I was told to quote a very high price, sometimes even higher than five hundred dollars for old, cracked, discolored show pieces which were neither unbreakable nor made of steel. On the contrary, they were very brittle. Unable to cheat people anymore, I came up with a plan. I started breaking the pieces which were too expensive in order to avoid cheating those poor white Canadians. It's on one of those breaking routines that my mama ji's friend's wife saw me and terminated me from the job without even paying the salary of one week and three days. In total, I earned eighty-five hundred dollars - forty-five hundred in the first three months and four thousand in the last two months.

Though I had earned very good money, more than anyone would have ever dreamt to earn in my entire family in just five months, my papa ji and mama ji were still not happy. Once I left the job at Best Antique Shop, I decided to take a sabbatical but everyone except me was against it. I wanted to sit at home and concentrate my entire energy on important things in life like internet chatting and watching videos but mama ji did not let me do that. Even mami ji, the wife of my mama ji, who till then had a relationship of avoidance with me, started pressuriszing me to get a new job.

While all this was disturbing me a lot, a big tragedy happened. Instead of papa ji, mummy ji passed away. I had always expected that to happen because she always prayed for her death than to live with a bad apple like papa ji but I did not expect that to happen when I was also contemplating to die. I returned to India three days after mummy ji's death, never to go back to Vancouver again. My mama ji also did not take much interest in calling me back because officially I was not related to him anymore with mummy ji not being around. God ji, unlike your Kans mama, who maintained relationship with you even after your mother's death, my mama ji changed his colors and severed all ties with the person who owed his name to him.

At My Home – Day VIII

Last Few Minutes Of My Life

God ji, if you still think that my name is not damaging enough for me to think of killing myself, I must let you know that my suffering mentioned till now are just the tip of the iceberg. There are so many vulgar incidents which I did not mention here because I fear that you might discontinue reading further. Incidents like my classmates painting a circle around a stray dog's ass with my name or me taken in police custody for a few minutes in Canada for telling a female police officer 'I Fuck, with you, in uniform your photograph."

These kind of incidents had become a normal part of my abnormal life. My harassment was not just restricted to my school, Sant Singh College or among friends but also in Gurudwaras in Canada where after a few visits I was ordered by mama ji not to take my name at the place of worship-the same mama ji who had once let my mummy ji assume that it was the name of some English God. There was not a single person other than the illiterates in my village who I was comfortable in telling my name. While old people turned their face on hearing my name, young people and kids felt amused. Despite having the complete knowledge of my name, everyone asked the meaning of my name. The problem was more with women than the men.

Today, I am dying as a pure virgin not because I have a damaged dirty-organ but because of my name. A young, smart and handsome man like me could have utilized my youth with a lot of good women-if not in India then at least in Canada but it never happened because the first thing those girls wanted to know when I approached them was my name and I never wanted to tell them that. God ji, the damage could have still been manageable and I might have postponed my death by a few years if there was no cable TV in the world but that also added ghee to the fire by educating more and more people about my name. God ji, I have seen people hiding their weaknesses in different ways and modern days' inventions have also helped them. However, there is no invention to help people with imperfect names.

God ji, you might think that I could have changed my name rather than end my life but you don't know today's world. This *kalyug* is very different from your *satyug* where anyone could have hundred names and one could use any of those as per one's convenience. I still don't understand how did you know if people were calling you or someone else because everyone had a different name for you. I really doubt if anyone ever called you by your real name

'Krishna', 'Ram' or 'Jesus' but you could manage to have so many different names because you did not have any birth certificate, voter id card, board result certificate, school leaving certificate, passport or even email ID. Trust me, God ji, it's easier for me to die and take rebirth again than get my name changed on all of these as it will not happen in one lifetime.

God ji, in these leftover minutes, I have to finish many important tasks. First, I have to paste the picture of my mama ji on the front wall under which I have to write with my blood 'Will see you in next life!' Then, I have the task of deciding something very important.

I have to decide how am I going to kill myself. I can't jump from my room's window and die because my room is on the ground floor. I can't ignite myself with fire because there is a strike of petrol pumps and ration depots, and there is neither kerosene oil at home nor diesel in the truck. I can't tie a rope on the fan and hang myself because the ceiling is already cracked and will not be able to take my seventy-six kilograms weight. I can't cut my wrist or throat because that will spoil the fashion quotient of my dead body. I can't think of consuming poison or pills because I am a habitual consumer of poison, courtesy the poisonous drinking water in Dangar Khera. Drowning is also not an option because other than the small dirty ponds, there is no river nearby for a swimmer like me to jump into and die. Finally, there is no traffic on the roads at this hour for me to die in an accident.

The only option left with me is to die by electric shock and I am well prepared for that. I have got a brand new wire, an old switch and a 'tried and tested' test-pin with me but there is no electricity. God ji, I have not asked anything from you in my illustrious life as I have achieved everything with my hard work. Today, when I am just a few moments away from meeting you, I pray to you to enlighten my room with electricity so that I die peacefully and leave this place for good.

God ji, I have just one word of advice before you read my suicide letter again. Please don't read it at night or you may end up feeling sleepy just like me. I would prefer you to read it during a rainy day so that your tears are mistaken for rain drops and your image of a composed, cool and *ghaint* personality is not spoilt.

God ji, though I don't have much to thank you for in my life but I would still do it because Gunjeet Madam taught us to end a letter with 'thank you' and I don't want to disappoint her even in my death.

God ji, thank you very much for these thirty-one years, one month, eight days, three hours and twenty-five seconds. God ji, if you are wondering that how could I count time so precisely all through my life without having a watch then I must tell you that it was possible because of my name. When one is Fuck, the only thing one can't go wrong with is time. After all fuck is all about time and time is all about fuck.

Good Morning.

Yours obediently,

Fuck Singh Brar

Son of both Sardar Makhan Singh and Late Harmeet Kaur ji

PS: Papa ji, I know you are a *harami* and despite my request on the envelope, you have opened and read this letter completely. I am sure that you have not understood anything because it's in English but you have still attempted reading it. I have only one last request. Please keep this letter in my dead body's shirt pocket while burning me so that it reaches God ji. Please don't keep it under the bed with used newspapers to sell it to Devi Dyal and make some money. Though you have not been nice to me but I would still wish something for you before I die-

May I become your father in next life. Amen!

About the Author

Harsh K Arora, born and brought up in small towns of Punjab, has been writing off and on for twenty years now. This is his first novel written on the basis of his experiences and observations of Punjab's hinterlands. In this book, he has tried to portray the spirited, carefree and fun filled picture of rural Punjab.

He has published a lot of short stories in leading regional newspapers and magazines and has been in the editorial panels of student magazines in his school and college days. Other than stories, he has got recognitions at University and Zonal levels in essay writings, caption contests, creative writings and elocutions.

He is a CFA Charterholder and has completed his MBA from IIT Delhi.

He is currently pursuing his entrepreneurial venture and is the Co-founder of Zvest Financial Services LLP. He is thirty-nine years old, married and settled in Bangalore for the last eight years. Apart from writing, he has a taste for a range of various other activities that he believes frees his mind and provides required impetus, thus constantly pushing his motivation level. He experiments and innovates continually to evolve along with time but never bypasses or overlooks the little joys of life. Global Economics is his passion, apart from cooking, swimming, traveling and reading.

www.ingramcontent.com/pod-product-compliance
Lightning Source LLC
LaVergne TN
LVHW041702070526
838199LV00045B/1172